English Words Formation

English Words Formation

Harmik Vaishnav

PRABHAT
PRAKASHAN

Published by
PRABHAT PRAKASHAN PVT. LTD.
4/19 Asaf Ali Road,
New Delhi-110 002 (INDIA)
e-mail: prabhatbooks@gmail.com

ISBN 978-93-5048-209-4
ENGLISH WORDS FORMATION
by Shri Harmik Vaishnav

Edition
2025

Price
₹ 500.00 (Rupees Five Hundred only)

Printed at
R-Tech Offset Printers, Delhi

"The Learner

in the

Reader of this book."

Preface

The verb is the centre of an English sentence construction. The words that are modified or changed in spelling take the shape of other parts of speech like Noun, Adjective and Adverb. This book compiles such parts of speech. A suffix or prefix is often used to modify the word into a different part of speech.

These parts of speech have different usage. E.g.

VERB	NOUN	ADJECTIVE
Amaze	amazement	amazing

- The grandeur of the Taj Mahal amazed the visitors
- The amazement of the child was seen from its face
- It is an amazing story.

Though the meaning is known there is often error in the usage of the right part of speech.

e.g. [N] danger [Adj.] dangerous

A sentence such as "Fire is danger" is often heard in colloquial language but the correct usage is "dangerous".

This book will be useful to understand the right use of word. The usage is explained with a sentence for understanding. It will be useful to students; aspirants of competitive exams, professionals and of course the lovers of English language.

Many words take affix to be formed form other part of speech.

Following affixes are routinely seen:

Suffix	Verb	Suffix	Verb
-e	Bathe	-ify	Simplify
-en	Shorten	Ise/ize	Realize/realize
-er	Glitter		

Suffix	Adjective	Suffix	Adjective
-able	Pitiable	-less	Fearless
-al	National	-like	Childlike
-ed	Learned	-ly	Friendly
-en	Golden	-ous	Dangerous
-ern	Southern	-some	Quarrelsome
-ful	Careful	-ward	Forward
-ible	Permissible	-worthy	Trustworthy
-ish	Childish		

Suffix	Adverb	Suffix	Adverb
-ly	Bravely	-ward	Upwards

Suffix	Noun	Suffix	Noun
-al	Arrival	-ment	Enjoyment
-ance	Observance	-ness	Darkness
-dom	Freedom	-red	Hatred
-ence	Dependence	-ship	Friendship
-er	Painter	-th	Growth
-hood	Childhood	-tion	Addition
-ion	Inspection	-y	Honesty

Verbs take prefixes from Nouns or Adjectives

Prefix	Verb	Prefix	Verb
-a	Arise	-in	Inlay
-ac	Accompany	-mis	Mistake
-be	Befool	-over	Overflow
-en	Encourage	-un	Undo
-for	Forgive	-under	Undergo
-fore	Foretell	-with	Withdraw

Contents

English Words Formation

A

VERB	NOUN	ADJECTIVE
Abandon	**abandonment**	**abandoned**

They abandoned the old building.

The social workers were touched, seeing the abandonment of the child.

Do not enter that abandoned building.

Abhor	**abhorrence**	**abhorrent**

We abhor crimes against women.

The lawyer was full of abhorrence for the atrocity committed.

What an abhorrent crime!

Abridge	**abridgement**	**abridged**

I will abridge the short story to explain to them.

The abridgement of the story was finely done.

The abridged article was published.

Absorb	**absorption** **absorbent**	**absorbing** **absorptive**

Cotton will absorb liquid.

The absorption of the chemical is taking lot of time.

The absorbent material was imported from Europe.

Abstract	**abstract**	**abstract**

I did not abstract the poem.
The abstract of the poem is not so good.
The abstract matter cannot be accepted.

Abuse	**abuse** **abuser**	**abusive**

Do not abuse anyone.
The abuser was paid in his own coin by the management.
I don't like abusive language.

Accept	**acceptance**	**acceptable**

Please accept this small gift.
Acceptance of a new idea is not easy.
Your proposal is acceptable to us.

Accommodate	**accommodation**	**accommodating**

Can you accommodate us in the car?
I am looking for a good accommodation for my family.
Everyone likes an accommodating person.

Accomplish	**accomplishment**	**accomplished**

The battalion accomplished the mission.
Your accomplishments are because of your efforts.
An accomplished artist should train others.

Accord	**accordance**	**accordant**

Try to accord with your neighbours.
If you live in accordance with the neighbours, life will be better.
An accordant person is admired.

Account	**account** **accountant**	**accountable**

I cannot account for his rude behaviour.
The account of the life of great men inspires us.
My father is an accountable person in the family.

Accumulate	**accumulation**	**accumulative**

Everyone wants to accumulate money.
There has been accumulation of stamps in the museum.
The accumulative amount can be used for the welfare.

Accuse	**accusation**	**accusatory**

Do not accuse anyone without proof.
The false accusation was proved soon.
Your accusatory remark hurts.

Ache	**ache**	**achy**

The injury will ache a lot.
Toothache is very painful.
The doctor advised to remove the achy tooth.

Acknowledge	**acknowledgement**	**acknowledged**

Please acknowledge this cheque.
The acknowledgement of the cheque should be in writing.
The acknowledged cheque was deposited in the bank.

Add	**addition** **addendum**	**additional**

Do not add water in it.
Addition of water will make it mild.
Remove the additional water from the vessel.

Adhere **adherence** **adhesive**

One must adhere to the system.

The adherence to the process will help in smooth working.

The adhesive tape is new.

Adjudicate **adjudication** **adjudicative**

The Chief Justice will adjudicate this matter.

The process of adjudication calls from tremendous thought and insight into the matter.

The adjudicative matter was put before the Chief Justice.

Adjust **adjustment** **adjustable**

You need to adjust yourself in the society.

The adjustment of the wheel was not easy.

Let us buy an adjustable glass for the car.

Administer **administration** **administrative**

The government administers our country.

The administration of our state is good.

New Delhi is the administrative capital of India.

Admire **admiration** **admiring**
admirable

I admire good work.

He has lot of admiration for you.

The admirable manager was promoted.

Admit **admission** **admissible**
admittance

Will the school admit poor children?
I got admission in a good college.
The argument was not admissible in the court.

Adopt **adoption** **adoptive**

They should adopt to the new ways of management.
The adoption process has much legality.
The adoptive professional can progress well and adjust well with everyone.

Adulterate **adulteration** **adulterant**
adultery

Do not adulterate the chemical by adding carbonate.
Adulteration in eatables is a severe crime.
The adulterant person cannot be trusted morally.

Advance **advancement** **advanced**

The army will advance at morning.
The advancement of the army took lot of planning.
The advanced money was returned to the bank.

Advise **advice** **advisable**

I would not like to advise anyone.
Your advice is helpful.
It is advisable to see the doctor for the ailment.

Affect **effect** **affecting**

The cold affected his health.
The effect of cold was not good for his health.
The affecting medicine should be taken regularly.

Affirm **affirmation** **affirmative**

It was affirmed when the great leader stated.
The judge's affirmation was respected by all.
I like your affirmative statement.

Affix **affix** **affixed**

Please affix the name plate outside.
The affix on the wall looks good.
The affixed photograph is tilted.

Agree **agreement** **agreeable**

Do you agree to this point?
The agreement was signed and dispatched.
The agreeable points were written in the minutes of the meeting.

Ail **ailment** **ailing**

What ails you?
The ailment is severe.
The ailing man was helped by an expert doctor.

Aim **aim** **aimless**

I will aim high.
My aim will not miss.
The aimless man just passes time.

Alarm	**alarm**	**alarming**

The roar of the lion alarmed the animals.
The alarm was given by the weather department.
It was an alarming experience.

Alert	**alert**	**alert**

I will alert the police.
An alert signal was given at the port.
An alert player noticed the error in the game.

Allege	**allegation**	**alleged**

He alleges that the prisoner was a spy.
Your allegation has no base.
The alleged man was proved innocent.

Ally	**ally** **alliance**	**allied**

England allied with the US in the Second World War.

The alliance of the US and the UK defeated Germany in Second World War.

The allied forces captured France from the enemies.

Alternate	**alteration**	**alternate**

Why did you not alternate this shirt with a new one?
How was the alteration done without machine?
The alternate plan was also discussed in the meeting.

Amaze	**amazement**	**amazing**

You will amaze all with your new hair style.
The amazement on the child's face was clearly visible.
The amazing story enthralled all.

Amuse **amusement** **amusing**

The children amuse themselves with toys.
The amusement park is near our home.
Where did you read this amusing story?

Anaesthetize **anaesthesia** **anaesthetic**

The surgeon had to anaesthetize the patient before operating.
The anaesthesia worked fast on the patient.
There cannot be any compromise in the quality of anaestheticdrug.

Analyse **analysis** **analytical**
analytic

Please analyse this balance sheet once.
The CEO's analysis about the new project were logical.
He has got an analytical brain.

Animate **animation** **animated**
animate

The kid animated some sounds on the stage.
The animation of the story was interesting.
The animated sounds baffled us.

Answer **answer** **answerable**

We would like to answer this query.
What is your answer for this query?
The answerable officer is on leave today.

Anticipate **anticipation** **anticipatory**

Do not anticipate a miracle every time.
He took this loan in anticipation of a hike in salary.
The anticipatory bail was not granted by the judge.

Ape **ape** **apish**

The naughty boy aped in the class.
The ape was caged and delivered in the zoo.
Your apish pranks will irritate the teacher.

Apologize **apology** **apologetic**

Why don't you apologize for this mistake?
The written apology was accepted.
His apologetic voice informed about his feelings.

Appeal **appeal** **appellate**

He should appeal in the High Court.
The appeal was rejected by the judge.
The appellate draft needs to be revised.

Apply **application** **applicable**

Have you applied for the said post?
The application has to be forwarded with the credentials.
The applicable law will be put before the judge.

Appreciate **appreciation** **appreciative**

I appreciate your hospitality.
The words of appreciation are enough to boost my morale.
Your appreciative gesture will be remembered by all.

Approach **approach** **approachable**

I approached him for a partnership.

The approach to the problem was not proper so there was not any solution.

The approachable gate to the ranch was broken.

Appropriate **appropriation** **appropriate**

Try to appropriate the statement.
Your appropriation about this case is good.
The appropriate person will be given due authority.

Approve **approval** **approved**

I do approve this budget.
The approval from the central government will take one month.
Where is the approved document?

Approximate **approximation** **approximate**

While budgeting for the project, try to approximate the raw material expenses.
In such projects the approximation may not always work out.
The approximate figure was reached after much deliberation.

Argue **argument** **argumentative**

Do not argue with your teacher.
The argument between the two lawyers lasted the whole day.
The argumentative spirit calls for logical reasoning and presence of mind.

Arm **arms** **armed**

The king armed his soldiers well.
The arms should be used very less.
The armed guards were posted out of the temple.

Ascend	**ascent** **ascension** **ascendancy**	**ascendant**

He will ascend the mountain without oxygen.

The ascent to the mountain was tough.

The people wanted to see the ascendant film star.

Aspire	**aspiration** **aspirant**	**aspirant**

I aspired to become an army officer.

His aspiration to become a judge made him study law.

The army aspirant candidates need to physically fit.

Assemble	**assembly** **assembler** **assemblage**	**assembled**

How many stamps did you assemble in your album?

The assembly of the stamps took 10 years of this hobby.

The assembled stamps were donated in the museum.

Assert	**assertion** **assertiveness**	**assertive**

He asserted his point with a valid proof.

I like his assertiveness.

The assertive person was promoted as manager.

Assess **assessment** **assessed**
assessor

The committee assessed the damage caused by the earthquake.

The assessment order was issued by the income tax commissioner.

The assessed balance sheet was submitted in the income tax office.

Assign **assignment** **assigned**
assigner

Whom will you assign this task?

The assignment was completed by the student on time.

The assigned task was done by me successfully.

Assimilate **assimilation** **assimilative**
Assimilator

Let us assimilate some students as volunteers of the programme.

The assimilation of the students today was pre-planned.

The assimilative students were addressed by the principal.

Associate **association** **associative**

Who will associate with you if you behave like this?

The association of the industries have requested the government to reconsider the tax matter.

The associative members will discuss about the programme.

Assume **assumption** **assuming**

The manager will assume that you are lying.

Your assumption about the new engineer is right.

He is not an assuming person.

Assure **assurance** **assured**

I assure you my support.
What is the assurance that this will not happen again?
The sum assured will be deposited in the bank.

Attain **attainment** **attainable**

Who can attain this tough target?
The attainment of success is the ultimate goal for a professional.
The attainable goal was analyzed.

Attract **attraction** **attractive**

The natural beauty of the region attracts everyone here.
There is attraction between the opposite poles of a magnet.
The new dress is attractive.

Attribute **attribution** **attributable**

I attribute this success to hard work.
Can you write an attribution for me?
The efforts put by him are attributable.

Audit **audit** **auditable**

Who will audit the accounts?
The bank audit will be over in a few days.
The expense account of the Governor of any state is not auditable.

Augment **augmentation** **augmentative**

We need expert engineers to augment this system.
Staff augmentation is a big challenge for the companies.
The augmentative steps were taken by the management for the betterment of the organization.

Authorize	**authorization** **authority**	**authoritative**

The collector of the district will authorize the document.
The collector has tremendous authority.
The judge spoke in an authoritative.

Avail	**avail** **availability**	**available**

How will you avail the loan?
The availability of the raw material is short-lived.
As per the available information, he is in town..

Avoid	**avoidance**	**avoidable**

Avoid bad company.
The avoidance of smoking improved his health.
Intoxication is completely avoidable.

❑

B

VERB	NOUN	ADJECTIVE
Back	**backing**	**backless**

My party will back me for the position.
You need a strong financial backing to start an industry.
The backless dress was not allowed in the school.

Balance	**balance**	**balanced**

You need to balance professional and personal life.
The balance of power was a well thought of strategy.
His balanced mind will give some good ideas in the time of crisis.

Ban	**ban**	**banned**

The government has banned the book.
Why did they lift the ban so fast?
The banned books were smuggled and sold at high price.

Banish	**banishment**	**banished**

The king will banish all those who work against the state.
The banishment of the bandits reduced the crime in the state.
Nobody is helping the banished criminals.

Bank	**bank**	**bankable**

Can I bank on you for advice?
The bank has decided to finance the project.
His attitude is bankable for the friends.

Bankrupt	**bankrupt**	**bankruptcy**

The recession has bankrupted many businessmen.
The bankrupt man finally committed suicide.
There is a legal proceeding to file bankruptcy.

Baptize	**baptism**	**baptismal**

They will baptize the child in church.
The baptism ceremony will last for one hour.
Conducting a baptismal ceremony needs training.

Bare	**bare**	**bare**

He will have to bare the leg to tie the bandage.
Don't live the wound bare.
The bare wound has swollen.

Base	**base**	**baseless**

He based his factory in his native.
The base of the building has to be strong.
The baseless argument was not discarded by the judge.

Batter	**batter**	**battered**

The lady battered the flour to prepare a delicacy.
Add sugar in that batter to make it sweet.
The battered flour was put in the oven for baking.

Bear	**bearer** **birth**	**bearable** **born**

The lioness will bear cubs soon.
The lioness gave birth to three cubs.
The newly born cubs are growing fast.

Beat	**beat** **beater**	**beatable**

The police will beat the criminal.
The beat on the back was painful.
The wheat has become soft and beatable.

Beautify	**beauty**	**beautiful**

The students will beautify the college for the annual event.
Natural beauty attracts all.
The beautiful dress was costly.

Befriend	**friendship**	**friend** **friendly**

I like to befriend sensitive and sensible people.
Our friendship is above self-interest.
A friendly person is welcome everywhere.

Beg	**begging** **beggar**	**beggarly**

The poor man will beg for food.
The blind beggar got no attention from the passers-by.
The beggarly cloths need to be removed from the collection.

Beguile **beguilement** **beguiling**

I would not beguile with empty words.

The beguilement of the poor folks with great promises is shameful.

The beguiling statements of the politicians need to be put under scanner.

Behave **behaviour** **behavioural**

The children behave well at home.

Your behaviour in the meeting was noticed by all.

He studies the behavioural patterns of the animals.

Believe **belief** **believable**
believer

I believe in what he says.

Gandhiji's belief in non-violence changed the history of India.

The statement made by the lawyer is believable.

Bend **bend** **bendy**

Do not bend the ruler, it will break.

The bend on the highway is dangerous.

It is difficult to drive on this bendy road.

Benefit **beneficiary** **beneficent**
beneficence **beneficial**

We benefit from the investment in bank.

The beneficiary will get a good amount.

The beneficial match was applauded by the crowd.

Better **betterment** **better**

I will better my speech next time.

Who works for the betterment of the masses?

Ram is better than Shyam in studies.

Bewilder **bewilderment** **bewildering**

You will bewilder the kids with your puzzle.
The bewilderment on the face of the public was visible.
The bewildering case was solved by the Chief Justice.

Bid **bidding** **bidder**

I cannot bid for this property.
The bidding went very high.

Bifurcate **bifurcation** **bifurcate**

Who will bifurcate the work among team members?
The bifurcation was mathematical and accepted by all.
The bifurcate work has to be completed by Sunday.

Billow **billow** **billowy**

The sail will billow once we are in open sea.
The boats floated on the billow of the sea.
The billowy tent was fastened again.

Bite **bite** **biting**

The dog will bite if you go near.
The bite of the cobra was fatal.
It is a biting cold today.

Blacken **black** **black**
blackness

Do not blacken the wall with smoke.
Black of the night near seashore is worthseeing.
The black coat was washed clean.

Blame	**blame**	**blameable**
		blameless
		blameworthy

Do not blame others for your mistake.
I will not take the blame on me.
His blameless personality is admired by all.

Blanket	**blanket**	**blanket**

The mist will blanket the hills at morning.
The blanket is warm and cosy.
The blanket hills are good to look at from far.

Blast	**blast**	**blast**

The soldiers will blast the bunker.
There was a powerful blast in the factory.
The blast case was transferred to the upper court.

Bleed	**blood**	**bloody**

The wound will bleed profusely.
Blood is scarce. Donate it.
In ancient times, there used to be bloody battles.

Blemish	**blemish**	**blemishing**

I will not blemish my image.
There is a blemish on the shirt.
The blemishing remarks were despised.

Bless	**blessing**	**blessed**

The parents blessed the couple.
We go to the temple for the blessing of God.
The blessed lives take birth as humans.

Blind	**blindness**	**blind**

The powerful light will blind the passers-by.

Milton's blindness did not stop him from becoming a great poet.

The blind man was helped by some children on the road.

Blink	**blinker**	**blinkered**

We blink eyes often.

The horse has to put on blinker for safety.

The blinkered eyes of horse saw nothing but the goal.

Bloom	**bloom**	**blooming**

The flowers will bloom in spring.

The bloom in the garden looked wonderful.

The blooming tree was a beautiful sight.

Bluff	**bluff**	**bluff**

Do not bluff in the interview.

His bluff was soon caught.

The bluff case was caught by the judge.

Blunt	**bluntness**	**blunt**

Over use has blunted the knife.

The bluntness in his words seemed rude.

The blunt sword does no harm.

Blur	**blur**	**blurred**

This glass will blur the light.

The blur is visible from afar.

The blurred photo cannot be sent to the press.

Bluster **bluster** **blustery**

Do not bluster with me like this.
The bluster had no effect on the hooligans.
The blustery sea was difficult to travel.

Boast **boast** **boastful**

He boasts of his riches.
The boast was paid in his own coin.
Your boastful nature will not fetch friends.

Boil **boil, boiler** **boiling**

Please boil water on stove.
The boiler is very big and costly.
The boiling water burnt his finger.

Bone **bone** **boneless**
bony

The old skeleton boned out of the coffin.
How many bones are there in human body.
This fish is boneless.

Boom **boom** **booming**

The market will boom during Diwali.
The boom in the diamond market is short-lived.
The booming economy of India is attractive to all.

Bootleg **bootlegger** **bootleg**

They may bootleg the alcohol to this town.
The bootlegger was caught by the police.
The bootleg material was seized by the police.

Bore	**bore**	**bored, boring**

Do not bore me with your poems.
He is such a bore.
The boring speech seemed too long to the students.

Boss	**boss** **bossiness**	**bossy**

He bossed around in his father's office.
The boss is always right.
Your bossy behaviour is harmful for team work.

Bother	**botheration**	**bothersome**

Who bother's to fight for the poor?
There is lot of botheration in running a company.
The bothersome problem was solved finally.

Bounce	**bounce** **bouncer**	**bouncy**

You cannot bounce the ball like this in a match.
The bounce went over the head of the batsman.
The bouncy pitch will not yield many runs for either side.

Brace	**brace**	**bracing**

The pillar will not brace the wall.
The braces were put under the ceiling.
Bracing pillars were not so strong.

Brand	**brand**	**branded**

We brand the company as we want.
Which is the most famous brand in clothes?
Do you buy branded shirts only?

Brave	**bravery** **braveness**	**brave**

The soldiers braved the enemy fortress.
He was rewarded for bravery.
The brave soldiers fought back the enemy.

Break	**breakage**	**breakable**

Do not break the glass.
The breakage in the ship can sink it.
It is a breakable item.

Brief	**briefness** **brevity**	**brief**

He will brief us in the meeting.
The brevity in the sentences will help us to understand better.
The brief meeting was purposeful.

Brighten	**brightness**	**bright**

A child in the house will brighten the day.
There is lot of brightness there, let us go there.
The bright boy won the medal.

Brim	**brim**	**brimful**

The pond will brim after the rain.
Do not fill the cup till the brim.
Take care of this brimful glass.

Broaden	**broadness** **breadth**	**broad**

They will broaden the roads.
Please reduce the breadth of the table.
The broad road is nice for driving.

Brood **brood** **broody**

Why do you brood on the same thing?
The brood of animals was fun to watch.
Your broody mind will give you stress.

Brown **brown** **brown, brownish**

The cobbler browned the shoes with colour.
Brown looks good in trousers.
The brownish shade looks good here.

Bubble **bubble** **bubbly**

Chemical bubbled on the surface.
Children like to play with bubbles.
The entire chemical was bubbly.

Budget **budget** **budgetary**

If you budget your expenses well you will have no problem.
The budget was proposed in the board's meeting.
There are certain budgetary constraints to this project.

Bulge **bulge** **bulgy**

If you do not exercise, your stomach will bulge.
The bulge in the bag looks funny.
Who will carry this bulgy bag?

Bump **bump** **bumpy**

I bumped into the wall unknowingly.
The bump on the road is not visible.
The bumpy road will harm the vehicle.

Buoy	**buoy** **buoyancy**	**buoyant**

How to buoy the mast is the question?
The buoyancy of the Indians is appreciable.
He has developed a buoyant nature.

Burden	**burden**	**burdensome**

Do not burden him more with extra work.
The burden was too much for the poor animal.
The burdensome matter was closed.

Burn	**burner**	**burning**

We can burn the waste paper.
The burner is made of metal.
The burning wood gave out heat.

Busy	**business**	**busy**

I will busy my employees with work.
What is your business here?
The busy man always finds time for doing something new.

❑

C

VERB	NOUN	ADJECTIVE
Calculate	**calculator**	**calculable**
	calculation	**calculated**

Will you calculate this sum for me?
Your calculation is perfect.
The sum is long yet calculable.

Calm	**calmness**	**calm**

We calmed the horse soon.
There is calmness everywhere in desert.
His calm nature solves many problems.

Cancel	**cancellation**	**cancelled**

I should cancel my visit.
The cancellation charges are not applicable.
Where is the cancelled cheque?

Care	**care** **careful**	**careless**

I care for all my friends.
Under whose care are the children now?
Her careless nature will be harmful.

Cause	**causality**	**causal** **causative**

Heat will cause many health problems.
There was no causality reported in the fire.
The causal action was replayed by the judge.

Caution	**caution**	**cautious** **cautionary**

I cautioned them against the electric current.
When did the weather department signal caution at the port?
Your cautious working style is good for safety.

Characterize	**characterization**	**characteristic**

I will characterize only five characters in this play.
How is the characterization in the plays of Shakespeare?
Diplomacy is the characteristic nature of Ram.

Charge	**charge**	**chargeable**

How will you charge for the consultation?
The electric charge is in the battery.
The chargeable battery is not costly.

Charm	**charm** **charmer**	**charming**

He has charmed the audience with his voice.
The snake charmer was playing with the snake.
Your charming personality attracts attention of many.

Cheapen **cheapness** **cheap**

Such behaviour will cheapen the image of the company.
Look at the cheapness in his conduct!
The cheap mangoes are not so good in taste.

Cheer **cheer** **cheerful**
cheerfulness

We cheer our players during the match.
Your brother's cheerfulness is admired by all the colleagues.
Child's cheerful nature is the centre of attraction.

Chew **chew** **chewy**
chewiness

You should chew the food well.
The chewiness in the food item was good.
The chewy gum is sweet.

Chill **chill** **chilly**

You will chill on the hills at this time.
One must experience the chill of the snowfall.
The chilly wind made us run home fast.

Chirp **chirp** **chirpy**
chirpiness

The birds chirp at morning.
The chirp of the little bird is sweet.
The chirpy voice of the singer is not to be considered for this song.

Choose **choice** **choosy**

Who will choose a shirt for me?
Your choice is good.
I am a choosy man.

Chum **chum** **chummy**
chumminess

He chums with all easily.
Ram is my chum.
The chummy relationship will not last long if you become selfish.

Circle **circle** **circular**
circulation

I will circle the page.
There are five marbles in the circle.
The circular route is easy to travel.

Circulate **circulation** **circulatory**

Please circulate this paper.
The circulation of English newspaper is more than Hindi newspaper.
The circulatory motion of the bike makes me feel dizzy.

Clang **clang, clangour** **clangourous**

Don't clang the bell.
The clang of the door was heard till far.
The clangourous sound of the machine is too loud.

Classify	**classification**	**classifiable**

How will you classify these items?
The classification of the items is based on the price.
The items are not classifiable on the price.

Clean	**cleanliness**	**clean**

Who will clean the table?
Cleanliness is next to Godliness.
The clean garden was a good sight.

Clear	**clearness**	**clear**

I will clear the mess.
The clearness in water will let you see the fish.
The clear water of the pond was refreshing.

Cloister	**cloister**	**cloistered**

The new monks were cloistered for learning.
Many monks live in the cloister.
The cloistered building is quite old.

Close	**closeness**	**close**

Please close the door.
The closeness of the insect to the body causes itching.
The close window is very dirty.

Cloud	**cloud** **cloudiness**	**cloudy** **cloudless**

Do not cloud your mind with negative thoughts.
The cloudiness of the day looks good.
The cloudy sky looked beautiful from the hills.

Coerce	**coercion**	**coercible, coercive**

Do not coerce the child like this.
Your coercion on them will not work.
The coercible manner of the boss is not welcomed.

Coexist	**coexistence**	**coexistent**

How do so many species coexist in the ocean?
Coexistence requires some type of mutual adjustments.
The coexistent animals were not removed from the zoo.

Coincide	**coincidence**	**coincident coincidental**

How did these two events coincide?
This happened due to the coincidence.
The coincident event failed.

Collect	**collection**	**collectable**

Please collect your cheque from here.
The collection of coins is a good hobby.
The collectable items were sold in the curio store.

Combat	**combat combatant**	**combatant combative**

I cannot combat so many men.
The combatant was trained in martial arts.
The soldiers showed combative mood during the battle.

Comfort	**comfort, comforter**	**comfortable**

I comforted him after his mother's death.
The comfort of the bed was nice after the journey.
This is not a comfortable pair of shoes.

Commemorate	**commemoration**	**commemorative**

How will you commemorate the great leader?
We erected the statue in his commemoration.
The commemorative speech was delivered by the chief guest.

Communicate	**communication**	**communicative**
	communicator	**communicatory**

I will communicate it to them.
You need to improve communication skills.
He teaches communicative Italian.

Commute	**commutation**	**commutable**

How do you commute to office daily?
The commutation will take 30 minutes.
It is a commutable distance.

Compact	**compactness**	**compact**

The computer will compact all the files.
The compactness has enabled more storage.
The compact phone is easy to put in pocket.

Compare	**comparison**	**comparative**

You should not compare yourself with others.
There is no comparison between man and God.
The comparative books are worth-reading.

Compel	**compulsion**	**compelling**

Why are you compelling the kids to do it?
There is no compulsion to do it.
The compelling situation was difficult to handle.
The soldiers behaved compellingly with the civilians.

Compensate	compensation	compensatory

The government will compensate the loss.
All the victims were paid compensation within one year.
The compensatory leave should be taken within forty-five days.

Compete	competition	competitive

Do not compete with others, but with self.
There is fierce competition among them.
I like your competitive mood.

Complement	complement	complementary

My wife complements my life.
Sugar is the complement to tea.
The complementary part was fitted well in the machine.

Complete	completeness completion	complete

Who will complete the work?
This sentence is the completeness of essay.
The complete work was submitted in the office.

Complicate	complication	complicated

Do not complicate the simple matter.
There are many complications in his health.
The complicated case was given to CID.

Compliment	compliment	complimentary

I complimented on his success.
Thanks for your compliment.
The complimentary gift was wonderful.

Compose	**composition**	**compositional**

You have composed good music.
The composition of the song took 5 days.
The compositional note was suggested by the expert musician.

Compound	**compound**	**compound**

Compound the two chemicals well.
The compound of the chemicals was added in water.
The compound mixture was heated.

Comprehend	**comprehension**	**comprehensible**

He could comprehend the matter fast.
The comprehension was of 10 marks.
The comprehensible report was submitted.

Compress	**compression**	**compressible**

Try to compress the clothes in the bag.
The compression of the air busted the machine.
It is a compressible chemical.

Computerize	**computer** **computerization**	**computerized**

Take a computerized print.
Computer has changed the world.
Computerized statement needs not sign on it.

Conceive	**conceivable**	**conceivably**

What idea did you conceive about it?
It is a conceivable matter of thought.
The thought process began conceivably.

Concern	**concern** **concernedness**	**concerned**

I am not concerned with him.

What is your concern?

The concerned friend ran for help.

Conciliate	**conciliation,** **conciliator**	**conciliatory**

You need to conciliate the baby.

This pact was done in conciliation of war.

The conciliatory agreement was drafted well.

Conclude	**conclusion**	**conclusive**

What do you conclude from his speech?

What is the conclusion of the case?

The conclusive statement by the judge was effective.

Concrete	**concrete** **concretion**	**concrete**

We will concrete the wall.

The concrete buildings are costly.

The concrete structure could not withstand the earthquake.

Concur	**concurrence**	**concurrent**

Do you concur to his statement?

The concurrence about the division of work was worked out in the meeting.

The concurrent work cannot be stopped.

Condemn **condemnation** **condemnatory**

God will condemn the sinner.
God's condemnation is slow but sure.
The condemnatory remarks against religion were taken seriously.

Condescend **condescension** **condescending**

The king condescends in public always.
The king's condescension was a blessing to the poor.
Your condescending behaviour is praiseworthy.

Condition **condition** **conditional**

You will have to condition your body as per the weather.
The condition of the poor is not good.
The conditional clause was removed from the agreement.

Confederate **confederate** **confederation** **confederate**

He confederated the group.
The confederation of retailers will meet the minister.
The confederate member enjoys many perks.

Confer **conferment** **conferrable**

Who conferred this title on him?
The official conferment was done in the presence of the President.
The title is conferrable on him.

Confess **confession** **confessional**

I confessed my mistake.
The father heard the confession.
The confessional statement of the criminal was recorded.

Confide	confidence confidant	confident

Can I confide in you?
Look at his confidence!
The confident man always wins.

Confirm	confirmation	confirmed

Please confirm your ticket.
The confirmation can be given on phone.
The confirmed pass was given to me.

Confiscate	confiscation	confiscated

The police will confiscate the bottles.
The case of confiscation of land was put before the judge.
The confiscated goods were auctioned by the government.

Conform	conformation	conformable

He conforms to all the rules of the company.
What is the conformation of this material?
He has a conformable nature.

Confront	confrontation	confrontational

Do not confront your boss.
Why should we avoid confrontation with everyone?
The confrontational meeting was finally convened by the Director.

Congratulate	congratulation	congratulatory

Did you congratulate him on his rank?
We accept your congratulation.
The congratulatory remark was heard by all.

Congregate	**congregation**	**congregational**

People will congregate in Church on Sunday.
The priest addressed the congregation.
The congregational address was well drafted.

Conjecture	**conjecture**	**conjectural**

Can you conjecture about the price of this house?
What shall we do at this conjecture?
The conjectural decision has to be taken by the manager.

Connect	**connection** **connector, connective**	**connectively**

Try to connect the dots.
There is no connection between him and the police.
I missed the connective flight.

Connote	**connotation**	**connotative**

The word connotes something.
I cannot understand the connotation of the sentence.
What is the connotative meaning of the word?

Conserve	**conservation** **conservator**	**conservative**

We should conserve forest.
Conservation of environment is the prime focus in the world.
The conservative approach is right.

Consider	**consideration**	**considered**

Please consider my application.
Your consideration is right.
The considered matter is promoted to the bench.

Consist **consistency** **consistent**

This chemical consists of water.
I like his consistency in work.
A consistent sportsman can win.

Console **consolation** **consolatory**

Who will console the crying child?
We wrote a note of consolation to the colleague.
The consolatory speech was delivered in the gathering.

Consolidate **consolidation** **consolidated**
consolidator

Please consolidate the matter and type it.
The consolidation of the case matter took lot of time.
Send me the consolidate report.

Conspire **conspiracy** **conspiratorial**
conspirator

Who can conspire against the country?
The conspiracy was unearthed by the police.
The conspiratorial brain has to be alert.

Constitute **constitution** **constituent**
constitutional

What constitutes bread?
The constitution of flour and water is used in making bread.
The constituent items were bought from the market.

Constrain **constraint** **constrained**

I constrained him to do the job again.
There are certain constraints in this matter.
The constrained workers had to work till late.

Construct	**construction**	**constructive**
	constructor	

Who will construct the building here?
The construction work has been delayed.
The constructive work was taken by the government.

Constrict	**constriction**	**constrictive**

Please constrict the cotton in this basket.
Constriction of cotton was not easy.
The constrictive cotton was packed well.

Consult	**consultancy**	**consultative**
	consultant	
	consultation	

Should I consult the doctor?
His consultancy fee is high.
The consultative charges do not include the visits.

Consume	**consumption**	**consumable**
	consumer	

Who consumed this much water?
Water consumption will rise in summer.
The consumable goods are sold fast.

Consummate	**consummation**	**consummate**

I will consummate the mission anyhow.
The consummation of such a goal is not easy.
The consummate goal was explained to the team.

Contemplate	**contemplation**	**contemplative**

Do not contemplate much about it?

We sat in contemplation of the case.

The contemplative mood of the poet was disturbed by the noise.

Content	**content** **contentment** **contented** **contentedness**	**contentedly**

Who can content the demon?

We sat in contentment after the meals.

The contented man is in peace with himself.

Continue	**continuation** **continuity**	**continuous**

I will not continue this work.

What did he say in continuation to the meeting yesterday?

The continuous sound disturbs us.

Contract	**contract**	**contractible**

We contracted for the new project.

What is written in the contract?

Is it a contractible disease?

Contradict	**contradiction**	**contradictory**

Why do you contradict me every time?

Your contradiction of the project perturbs me.

The two statements are contradictory.

Contribute	**contribution**	**contributory**
	contributor	

How can I contribute in this work?
What is your contribution in this project?
The contributory work helped a lot.

Contrive	**contrivance**	**contrived**

I contrived to get it done.
The contrivance of project calls for great skills.
It was a contrived report.

Control	**control, controller**	**controllable**

Who will control the dog?
Do not lose control of you speech.
The flight is not controllable.

Controvert	**controversy**	**controversial**

He will not controvert about the new bill.
There is a great controversy in this bill.
The controversial remark stirred the nation.

Converge	**convergence**	**convergent**

The rivers converge near the sea.
The convergence of two companies is good for business.
The convergent force helped the business to progress.

Converse **conversation** **conversational**

I converse in English.
It was a wonderful conversation about life.
You taught you conversational techniques.

Convert **conversion** **convertible**
convertibility

I can convert this chemical.
The conversion process of the chemical is long.
The chemical is not convertible.

Convey **conveyance** **conveyable**
conveyor

Please convey this message.
The conveyor belt on the airport was not working.
The conveyable goods were brought in van.

Convince **conviction** **convincible**
convincing

I cannot convince my father.
Gandhiji had a strong conviction about freedom.
It is not a convincing statement.

Convulse **convulsion** **convulsive**

He convulsed the jar with a heavy hand.
There is convulsion in my stomach.
The convulsive movement of the muscles is the cause of injury.

Cool	**coolness**	**cool**

How will you cool the water?
The coolness of the place is very soothing.
Have some cool water.
He behaved coolly during the crisis.

Co-operate	**co-operation**	**co-operative**

Will you co-operate with us for this project?
We thank you for your co-operation.
Your co-operative nature can get the work done.

Co-opt	**co-option**	**co-optive**

I will not co-opt for him in the project.
The co-option of Ram was correct.
It is not a co-optive position.

Correct	**correction** **corrector** **correctional** **correctness**	**correctly**

Please correct the sentence.
The correction of the papers took long.
The correctional measures need to well planned.

Correlate	**correlation**	**correlative**

How do you correlate these two incidents?
The correlation of two incidents is interesting.
The correlative part was fitted well.

Correspond	**correspondence** **correspondent**	**corresponding**

The line A corresponds to line B.
Is there any correspondence between them?
The corresponding piece was found out from the junk.

Corroborate	**corroboration** **corroborator**	**corroborative**

We should corroborate with our group company.
This corroboration is working wonders in the project.
The corroborative efforts of the management yielded results fast.

Corrode	**corrosion**	**corrosive**

Rain will corrode the road.
There is some corrosion in the machine.
Anti-corrosive material was spread on the tank.

Corrupt	**corruption** **corruptibility** **corruptness**	**corrupt** **corruptible** **corruptive**

The system will corrupt the new recruits soon.
Corruption is a big problem in the country.
The corrupt officials should be punished severely.

Cost	**costing**	**costly**

What will this gift cost us?
The cost of the gift is not much.
The costly vase was placed in the drawing room.

Count	**count counting**	**countable**

Do not count your chickens before they are hatched.
How much is the head count after the recruitment drive?
The countable items are placed on the table.

Counter	**counter**	**counter**

Do not counter your boss.
Army's counter was powerful.
The counter attack soon subsided.

Counterfeit	**counterfeit**	**counterfeit**

He can counterfeit any sign.
The counterfeit mechanism was caught.
The counterfeit coins were recovered from the smuggler.

Cover	**cover, coverage**	**covered**

Please cover the child, it is cold.
The report has a vast coverage.
There are some covered plates there.

Covet	**covetous**	**covetously**

The greedy landlord coveted to take his land.
His covetous attitude has landed him into trouble.
He spoke covetously of the neighbouring land.

Crackle	**crackle**	**crackly**

The door will crackle a bit when you open.
The crackle was heard in another room.
The crackly door needs repairing.

Cramp **cramp** **cramped**

Do not cramp their progress with rules and regulations.
There is a cramp in my leg.
The cramped street is crowded.

Crash **crash** **crashing**

He crashed the bike against the wall.
The noise of plane crash was heard many miles away.
The crashing sound was heard till far.

Creak **creak** **creaky**

The window creaks a lot.
Listen to the creak of the door in the next room.
The creaky sound at night was frightening.

Cream **cream, creaminess** **creamy**

The cook creamed the dessert.
Wow! Look at the creaminess of the cake.
The creamy cake was soon consumed by the kids.

Create **creation, creativity creativeness, creator** **creative**

I would like to create a new design.
This is the creation of a great artist.
Your creative mind can imagine some design.

Credit **credit credibility** **credible creditable**

The whole amount was credited in her account.
The project was given because of his credit.
The performance was creditable.

Creep	**creep, creepiness**	**creepy**

The thief will creep in at night.
There is creepiness in the film.
I heard a creepy ghost story.

Croak	**croak, croakiness**	**croaky**

A bull frog was croaking at a distance.
The croak was loud and clear.
The children made croaky noise.

Crook	**crook, crookedness**	**crooked**

I crooked my thumb to pick up the cup.
There is crookedness in his walk.
The crooked guy was punished by the people.

Crowd	**crowd, crowdedness**	**crowded**

The youngsters crowded the fair.
There was a big crowd near the hall.
I do not like the crowded place.

Crumble	**crumble**	**crumbly**

I crumbled the pieces of paper.
The British Empire began to crumble.
The crumbly structure will be restored.

Crunch	**crunch, crunchiness**	**crunchy**

He crunched the cash flow.
There is severe crunch of gold in the market.
The crunchy wafers are good to eat.

Cry	**cry, crying**	**crying**

Who is crying?
The baby's crying was heard at night.
The crying baby was pacified by the mother.

Cube	**cube**	**cubic**

Five cubed is 125.
What is the cube of 10?
Cubic meters were calculated quickly.

Cuddle	**cuddle**	**cuddly**

The child cuddled near the mother.
I took my kid in a tight cuddle.
It is a cuddly teddy bear.

Cultivate	**cultivation cultivator**	**cultivated, cultivable**

We will cultivate two crops this year.
The cultivation of wheat requires lot of water.
The cultivable land should not be used for factory purpose.

Cure	**cure, curability**	**curable**

Who cured me?
The cure was not easy.
Now malaria is a curable disease.

Curl	**curl, curler, curliness**	**curly**

The smoke curled upwards.
The little girl's curls were pretty.
You should maintain your curly hair.

Curse **curse** **cursed**

The saint cursed the naughty boy.

The curse on Ahaliya was removed with the effect of Lord Ram.

The cursed forest is a terrible sight.

Cut **cut** **cutting**

Do not cut the vegetables like this.

There is a deep cut on his hand.

The cutting remark of the girl subdued the boy.

❑

D

VERB	NOUN	ADJECTIVE
Damage	**damage**	**damaged**

Do not damage the monument.
The plant suffered a great damage in the cyclone.
The damaged goods were replaced by them.

Damn	**damn, damnation**	**damnable**

I damned him for such an act.
The damnation fell like the thunderbolt on the demon.
It is a damnable act.

Dampen	**dampness**	**damp**

Please dampen this cloth for me.
The dampness in the chemical will spoil it.
The damp cloths are not comfortable to wear.

Dance	**dance, dancer**	**danceable**

Will you dance with me in the party?
The dancer practised much before performing on the stage.
The danceable songs were played at the function.

Dare	**dare, daring**	**daring**

He will not dare to talk to me like that again.

The daring deed of the commando helped in catching the terrorist.

The daring dog helped in catching the culprit.

Darken	**dark** **darkness** **darkener**	**dark, darkish**

It will darken in a while.

As the darkness descended on the hills, all was silent.

The dark shirt will look good.

Dash	**dash**	**dashing**

The guard dashed out to catch him.

He hit the door in dash.

The dashing young man was selected for the position.

Date	**date**	**dated**

He will date his meeting well.

What date is it today?

The proposed function is not dated.

Dazzle	**dazzle**	**dazzling**

The light will dazzle the animals.

The dazzle because of the light resulted into an accident.

The dazzling star was applauded.

Deafen	**deafness**	**deaf**

Your horn deafens me.

The doctor is trying to cure his deafness.

The deaf man was given a hearing aid.

Debate	**debate**	**debatable**

Why do you debate with your colleagues on this matter?
What was the outcome of the debate?
The debatable matter was heard by the judge patiently.

Decay	**decay**	**decayed**

The fruits will decay soon.
The decay was due to lack of sunlight.
The decayed tooth has to be removed.

Decide	**decision**	**decisive**
		decidable, decided

Let us decide about this programme.
What is the decision of the manager?
The decisive point was ultimately taken into consideration.

Declaim	**declamation**	**declamatory**

The leader declaimed a few words before commencing the mission.

The declamation of the leader created a good impact.

Gandhiji's declamatory words stirred the spirit of the people of India.

Declare	**declaration**	**declarative**
	declarer	**declaratory**

The university will declare the result soon.
The declaration of the new budget was hailed by the people.
The declarative remarks were not understood.

Decline	**declension, declination**	**declinational**

I declined his offer.

The declension of Mughal Empire is because of many reasons.

The declinational stroke on the Mughal Empire was hit by the British.

Decorate	**decoration**	**decorative**

Who will decorate this hall?

The decoration of the hall is a costly affair.

There are many decorative items available.

Decrease	**decrease**	**decreasing**

The government needs to decrease the spending on administration.

The decrease was taken as a corrective measure.

Dedicate	**dedication dedicator**	**dedicate dedicatory**

I dedicated my book to my best friend.

The dedication should be written on the front page.

The dedicatory speech of Nehru was full of sentiments.

Deduce	**deduction**	**deducible**

The police deduced on the clues available.

The deduction of Sherlock Holmes was always perfect.

What are the deducible points in this case?

Deduct	**deduction**	**deductible** **deductive**

Let us not deduct anything at this juncture.
There is a thought process in the deduction of the judge.
All the points are not deductible.

Deepen	**depth**	**deep**

The pit will deepen as the machine goes in.
What is the depth of the Pacific Ocean?
There was a deep pit in the ground.

Defame	**defamation**	**defamatory**

How can he defame me like that?
The defamation case was fought in the High Court.
Please take back your defamatory remarks.

Defeat	**defeat, defeatism**	**defeatist**

We shall defeat the rival team.
He could not bear the defeat and left the place.
You need to change your defeatist attitude.

Defend	**defence, defender** **defencelessness**	**defenceless**

How will you defend the fort with so less soldiers?
I would like to work in defence services.
Do not attack the defenceless person.

Defer	**deference**	**deferential** **deferentially**

The project was deferred by the Government.
I hold him in deference.
His deferential behaviour towards the teachers is admirable.

Define	**definition**	**definable**

Please define 'Verb'.
What is the definition of 'Noun'?
This term is not definable.

Deflate	**deflation**	**deflationary**

The thorn deflated the tyre.
The deflation of the economy is due to dumping.
The Government will have to remove the deflationary steps.

Deform	**deformation** **deformity**	**deformed**

The accident deformed the car.
The deformity in the machine has to be removed.
All the deformed parts of the car were removed.

Defy	**defiance**	**defiant**

Do not defy the order of the boss.
The freedom fighter stood in defiance with Gandhiji.
The defiant employee was sacked.

Degrade	**degradation**	**degrading**

You should not degrade anyone like this.
The degradation of the quality is due to bad raw material.
The degrading quality was studied by the experts to take corrective measures.

Delay	**delay**	**delayed**

We should not delay the project now.
What is the reason of this delay?
The delayed project went in loss.

Delete	**deletion**	**deleted**

Can I delete this line?
Deletion of this file is not possible.
How can I recover the deleted files?

Deliberate	**deliberation**	**deliberate** **deliberative**

Let us deliberate on the matter with team-mates.
The deliberation on the subject will take lot of time.
The deliberate efforts yielded good result.

Delight	**delight**	**delighted** **delightful**

How do you delight yourself with minimum money?
The delight was seen on the face of the child.
It was a delightful experience.

Delude	**delusion**	**delusive** **delusory**

Please do not delude the students.
They tourists are in delusion about the place.
The delusory plan was soon unearthed by the HR Manager.

Demand	**demand**	**demanding**

We cannot demand more and more all the time.
How is the demand of sugar nowadays?
The demanding nature of the manager is creating panic among the employees.

Demonstrate	**demonstration**	**demonstrative** **demonstrable**

The professor will demonstrate the experiment in the class.

The demonstration will take at least 2 hours.

The demonstrative methods are useful for teaching technical subjects.

Demoralize	**demoralization**	**demoralized**

Your remarks will demoralize the children.

There is tremendous demoralization among the employees.

The demoralized employee cannot perform well.

Depart	**departure** **department**	**departed**

They will depart at evening.

The departure if after 10 minutes.

The departed brothers met after many years.

Depend	**dependence** **dependability**	**dependable**

Whom do you depend on for this project?

By starting to earn, she has reduced the dependability on the family.

How many dependable members are there in your family?

Deplore	**deplorable**	**deplorably**

The public deplored the act of the terrorists.

The deplorable behaviour should not be tolerated.

I spoke deplorably about the calamity.

Deprecate **deprecation** **deprecatory**

I deprecate this type of work.

His deprecation has reached hatred.

The deprecatory remarks on the beloved leader were not liked by the public.

Depreciate **depreciation** **depreciatory**

It will soon depreciate.

How much depreciation do you foresee in real estate?

The Government is taking depreciatory steps against the inflation.

Depress **depression** **depressed**
depressive
depressing

This movie will depress you.

For depression, please meet the psychiatrist.

Your presence changed my depressed mood.

Deprive **deprivation** **deprived**
deprival

I shall not deprive my child from these good things.

The poor are suffering from deprivation.

The deprived class will rise one day.

Deride **derision** **derisive**
derisory

Other children derided him.

The derision in the class made him upset.

The boss's derisive statement created no effect on him.

Derive	**derivative**	**derivative**

What do you derive from this experience?
The derivative was well made.
The derivative figure was not correct.

Descend	**descent**	**descendant**

When will the mountaineers descend?
The descent was not as easy as it looked.
Who was the descendant of Akbar?

Describe	**description**	**descriptive**

Please describe the problem.
The description of the fort in words is marvellous.
It is a descriptive answer.

Desert	**deserter** **desertion**	**deserted**

You should not desert him.
He is deserter of friends.
The deserted village was found by the explorer.

Deserve	**deserving**	**deservedly**

He deserves a medal.
The deserving team will win.
He was awarded deservedly.

Design	**design, designer**	**designing**

Will you design a dress for me?
The designer got the national award for the best designing.
The designing team will work till late today.

Designate	**designation**	**designated**

Whom do you designate to do this job?
What is your new designation?
The designated officer was given a car with driver.

Desire	**desire**	**desirable**
	desirability	**desirous**
	desirableness	

I do not desire to do this now.
One cannot complete all the desires.
It is a desirable award.

Desolate	**desolation**	**desolate**
	desolated	**desolateness**

The young man desolated the old parents.
The old man had a nervous breakdown due to desolation.
The desolate island is very beautiful.

Destroy	**destruction,**	**destructively**
	destroyer destructive	
	destructible	

Who destroyed the building?
The earthquake caused tremendous destruction.
His destructive mind can think of such a wicked plan.

Detach	**detachment**	**detachable**

Please detach the speakers from the TV.
An amount of detachment from material things is required.
There are two detachable speakers in it.

Detail	**detail**	**detailed**

He is detailing his plan to the committee.
What detail did you get from the computer?
The detailed plan was submitted to the Government.

Detect	**detection** **detector**	**detectable**

It could detect some virus in the computer.
Police make wide use of lie detector now.
The case is detectable by an expert investigator.

Determine	**determination**	**determined**

The chairman will determine the price of the new machine.
You cannot achieve without determination.
The determined youth was spotted by the mentor.

Detest	**detestation**	**detestable**

detest you for doing such a thing.
He hit the man in detestation.
They should be severely punished for detestable crime.

Devastate	**devastation**	**devastating**

The storm devastated the whole area.
The devastation by the tsunami was beyond imagination.
A devastating tsunami hit the coastal area.

Develop	**development** **developer**	**developing** **developmental**

You should develop your personality well.
The development in the area is due to the new government.
The developing countries have a long way to go still.

Deviate	**deviation** **deviance** **deviancy**	**deviant**

Do not deviate from your path.
This deviation from the plan will be costly.
The deviant member of the committee was asked to resign.

Devote	**devotion**	**devote**

How much time can you devote for this work?
Your devotion in the work is good.
The devote man can do well.

Diagnose	**diagnosis**	**diagnostic**

The doctor will diagnose the disease after the report.
The diagnosis was perfect.
The HR people use some diagnostic tools to improve the culture of the company.

Dictate	**dictation** **dictator**	**dictatorial**

I will dictate the letter to the steno.
The children have dictation test.
I do not like your dictatorial behaviour.

Die	**death**	**deathly**

The old elephant will die in a few days.
The death of the leader is a severe blow on the party.
The deathly disease needs to be cured soon.

Diet	**diet, dieter**	**dietary**

I will diet for a few days to lose weight.
The diet was nourishing.
The dietary chart is displayed on that board.

Differ	**difference**	**different**

I differ in this matter.
What is the difference between noun and adjective?
The two brothers are quite different.
You should solve this problem differently.

Diffuse	**diffusion**	**diffusible** **diffusive**

They diffused the bomb.
The diffusion of the tense situation required tremendous tact.
It is not a diffusible bomb.

Digest	**digestion**	**digestive** **digestible**

The child cannot digest this heavy food.
His digestion has improved after he started exercising.
Your digestive system is strong.

Dignify	**dignity**	**dignified**

The attire dignifies his personality.
We should take care of the dignity of the profession we are in.
His dignified conduct impressed all.

Dim	**dimness**	**dim**

The light dimmed over the hills.
Can you see anything in this dimness?
The dim room was a scene to look at.
I remember him dimly.

Direct	**direction** **director** **directness**	**directive** **directional**

Who will direct us to the spot?
The director of the play is hard task master.
There are some directive principles for managers in this book.

Dirty	**dirt** **dirtiness**	**dirty**

The child dirtied the floor.
Please clean the dirt from the kitchen first.
Why don't you discard this dirty bag?

Disable	**disability, disablement**	

The lack of authority disabled the committee.
For him, disability is not a hurdle to do anything.

Disagree	**disagreement**	**disagreeable**

I disagree in this matter.
What is the disagreement about?
Your disagreeable nature is not good to keep relations.

Disappointment	**disappointment**	**disappointed** **disappointing**

Please don't disappoint me.
The loss in the firm is a matter of disappointment.
The disappointed employee resigned from the job.

Disarm	**disarmament**	**disarming**

The policed disarmed the burglar.

The international policy of disarmament did not get the desired result.

Disarming the poor of their rights is a sin.

Disbelieve	**disbelief**	**disbelievingly**

I disbelieve that cunning guy.
Why this disbelief about him?
He heard the case disbelievingly.

Discern	**discernment**	**discernible**

Can you discern between the twins?
The manager's discernment was right.
If it is a discernible matter, we don't have to worry.

Discipline	**discipline**	**disciplinary**

You need to discipline the cadets.
What is the importance of discipline in life?
We will have to take some disciplinary actions against them.

Disconnect	**disconnection**	**disconnected**

The water body will disconnect the forest and the mountain.
There is no disconnection between us.
The disconnected island got help finally.

Discontinue	**discontinuance**	**discontinuous**
	discontinuity	

Let us discontinue this practice.

The discontinuity of the medicine has created health problem again.

The discontinuous movement of machine is not good.

Discriminate	**discrimination**	**discriminatory**

I do not discriminate between my two sons.

There should not be discrimination on the basis of religion.

The discriminatory remark of the politician created tension in the town.

Disdain	**disdain**	**disdainful**

Why did you disdain him?

His disdain for the kid is not good.

Our disdainful comment was not lost on him.

Disgrace	**disgrace**	**disgraceful**

Your behaviour disgraced us all.

What a disgrace to fail like this!

The disgraceful manner should be punished.

Disgust	**disgust**	**disgusting**

Do not disgust me.

We stood there in disgust of the man.

That film was disgusting.

Dishonour **dishonour** **dishonourable**

Do not dishonour the order of the king.
The exiled minister could not bear the dishonour.
Why do you work with such a dishonourable man?

Dismay **dismay** **dismal**

My failure in exam dismayed my father.
It is dismay to lose the match like this.
They live in a dismal condition.

Dismiss **dismissal** **dismissive**

The judge will dismiss the petition.
His dismissal proved to be disastrous for the management.
The dismissive statement was given by the judge.

Disobey **disobedience** **disobedient**

Why do you disobey the boss?
Your disobedience of this rule is a crime.
The disobedient student will be punished.

Dispense **dispensation** **dispensable**

The salesmen will dispense the medicines.
The dispensation took a long time owing to queue.
The dispensable items were discarded.

Disperse **dispersion** **dispersive**
dispersal

Police dispersed the crowd.
The dispersion of the crowd called for mounted police.
The officers made dispersive moves.

Dispose	**disposal**	**disposable**

I will dispose the waste.

The chemical disposal in the river created many environmental problems.

Always use disposable syringes.

Dispute	**dispute** **disputant** **disputation**	**disputable** **disputatious**

We should not dispute for this.

The dispute was solved by the arbitrator.

The disputable parts of the speech should be removed.

Disrupt	**disruption**	**disruptive**

They disrupted the meeting.

Lord Ram saved the ashram from disruption.

Their disruptive acts were punished.

Dissent	**dissenter** **dissent**	**dissentient**

Will dissent the bill?

The dissenters were asked to leave.

The dissentient member was given notice.

Distract	**distraction**	**distracted**

He distracted me in the work.

Be away from distraction when working.

The distracted animals will attack the tourists.

Disturb	**disturbance**	**disturbed**

Who is disturbing them?
There is lot of disturbance because of loudspeaker.
The disturbed child started to cry.

Diverge	**divergence**	**divergent**

Two roads diverged into the woods.
There is no divergence from the plan.
The divergent views were respected by the head.

Divert	**diversion**	**diverting**
		diversionary

I will divert the car that side.
There is a diversion on the road.
The diverting roads will meet somewhere.

Divide	**division**	**divisional**
	divisibility	**divisible**

Please divide the chocolates among the children.
What was the reason for the division of property?
The divisible amount can be calculated easily.

Divorce	**divorce, divorcee**	**divorced**

He divorced his quarrelsome wife.
The court ordered the divorce.
The divorced man left the country.

Document	**document** **documentation**	**documentary**

Have you documented everything?
We need to have training on documentation in our company.
The documentary evidence was produced in the court.

Dodder	**dodder**	**doddery**

The tower doddered on the roof.
The dodderer needs to be strong.
The doddery tower fell on the ground because of heavy wind.

Domesticate	**domestication** **domesticity**	**domestic**

Man domesticated many animals.
The domestication of some animals is not possible.
Cow is a domestic animal.

Doom	**doom**	**doomed**

Trouble doomed on him.
If it is in doom it will happen.
The doomed ship had no survivors.

Dot	**dot**	**dotted**

Can you dot the map?
There are many dots on the paper.
Colour the dotted line.

Double	**double**	**double**

He doubled the profit in a few months.
The double of this is the target.
The double board is useful in classroom.

Doubt	**doubt** **doubtfulness** **doubtless**	**doubtful**

I doubted his credentials.
There is no doubt about it.
The doubtful product was removed.

Doze	**doze**	**dozy**

He will doze after the lunch.
A doze is required to refresh me.
The dozy boy was asked to go out of the class.

Dread	**dread**	**dreaded** **dreadful**

I do not dread the dark.
What is the dread among the sheep?
The dreadful beast was seen at night.

Drink	**drink, drinker**	**drinkable**

Can I drink some water?
Take a drink with me.
The tea is drinkable.

Drizzle	**drizzle**	**drizzly**

It drizzled at night.
The drizzle looked beautiful from far.
The drizzly weather was worth going out.

Droop	**droop, drooping**	**droopy**

He drooped near the gate.
The drooping will create pain in the back.
The droopy old man was helped by me.

Dry	**dryness**	**dried**

We dried the cloths in sunlight.
There is dryness in the area.
The dried land cannot be cultivated.
He spoke dryly about his love affair.

Dull	**dullness, dullard**	**dull**

The sunlight has dulled the colour on the wall.
Why is there dullness on his face?
The dull boy was counselled by the teacher.

Duplicate	**duplication** **duplicator**	**duplicate**

How did you duplicate this item?
There is no duplication in our product.
The duplicate sign was caught by the cashier.

❑

E

VERB	NOUN	ADJECTIVE
Eat	**eater**	**eatable**

I will eat this ice-cream.
The young man is a good eater.
The eatable bread needs to be buttered.

VERB	NOUN	ADJECTIVE
Edit	**edit, edition, editor**	**editorial**

How will you edit this report?
The second edition of my book has come out.
The editorial board will be responsible for the final print.

VERB	NOUN	ADJECTIVE
Educate	**educability** **education** **educative** **educable** **educator**	**educated**

We should educate our children well.
How the education in your state?
She will marry an educated boy only.

Elect **election** **elective**

We will elect an able leader.
When is the next election?
The elective person was asked many questions.

Elevate **elevator, elevation** **elevated**

He will elevate his relatives in the company.
We can go in elevator.
The elevated part of building was maintained well.

Elongate **elongation** **elongated**

Do not elongate this bag more.
The elongation of the item depends on the elasticity of the material.
The elongated rubber band will hurt if released suddenly.

Elucidate **elucidatory** **elucidation**

Please elucidate this formula.
Your elucidation of the chemical reaction is not right.
The elucidatory speech was given by the scientist.

Elude **elusion** **elusive**

I don't want to elude law.
Elusion of law is not good for democratic set-up.
The politician's elusive work is bad.

Emasculate **emasculation** **emasculate**

Gandhiji opposed the Rowlatt Act because it emasculated the Indian people.
Emasculation is a bad tactic used by management.
The emasculate man cannot perform well.

Embarrass **embarrassment** **embarrassed**

His behaviour in the party embarrassed us all.
I pray God to keep me away from the acts of embarrassment.
The embarrassed boy left the place immediately.

Embrace **embrace** **embraceable**

He embraced his friend.
I took my child in tight embrace due to wind.
The teddy bear is embraceable.

Emerge **emergence** **emergent**

A pride of Lion emerged from the bush.
The emergence of the new law has created worry in public.
Ram is the emergent leader of the party.

Emigrate **emigration** **emigrating**
emigrant

He emigrated to the Middle East.
They are emigrants from India.
The emigrating policy will be revised.

Employ **employment** **employable**
employer

How many workers did you employ?
There are many employment opportunities in the technical field.
The company is looking for some employable people.

Empty **emptiness** **empty**

I emptied the bucket of water on him.
The emptiness in the room causes echo.
Give me the empty bottles.

Emulate **emulation** **emulative**
emulator

The child emulates the father.
The emulation was exact.
The emulative acting is entertaining.

Enact **enactment** **enactive**

We will enact a comedy play.
The enactment of such a play calls for dramatic skills.
The enactive play is rehearsed well.

Enchant **enchantment** **enchanting**

The beauty of the Himalayas enchants everyone.
He has not come out of the enchantment of the beauty of the place.
The enchanting hills are worth visiting once.

Enclose **enclosure** **enclosed**

She will enclose a cheque in the parcel.
The sheep were kept in an enclosure at night.
The enclosed area was guarded by soldiers.

Endow **endowment** **endowed**

The old man was endowed with life time achievement award.
Insurance companies give endowment policies.
The endowed man can only create masterpieces.

Endure **endurance** **endurable**

The kids cannot endure the cold.
You have good endurance.
The heat in May is not endurable.

Enforce	**enforcement** **enforcer**	**enforceable**

The government will enforce the new rule.
The enforcement of the traffic rules calls for honest policemen.
We must think of only enforceable rules.

Engage	**engagement**	**engaged**

How will you engage the children in vacation?
I could not attend the function because of an engagement with the client.
The engaged couple got blessings.

Enjoy	**enjoyment**	**enjoyable**

Enjoy every moment of your life.
What is life without enjoyment?
Thanks for an enjoyable picnic.

Enlarge	**enlargement**	**enlarged**

The builder will enlarge the house.
The enlargement of the city limits is not easy.
The enlarged area will be protected by the army.

Enlighten	**enlightenment**	**enlightened**

The saint enlightened the people.
Lord Buddha got enlightenment under a tree.
The enlightened speaker is going to deliver a lecture.

Enrage	**rage**	**raging**

This act enrages me.
He attacked the thieves in rage.
The raging bull hit the dog.

Enrich	**enrichment** **richness**	**rich**

The lottery enriched the poor labourer.

He shows his richness in spending.

The rich do not worry about small matters.

Entertain	**entertainment** **entertainer**	**entertaining**

How will you entertain the guests?

The entertainment was wonderful.

I still remember that entertaining evening.

Entice	**enticement**	**enticing**

Do not entice the children with chocolates.

The children complete the homework fast due to enticement of chocolates.

The enticing ice-cream advertisement brought us here.

Entrench	**entrenchment**	**entrenched**

The soldiers entrenched some tunnels.

The entrenchment of the tunnel took several days.

The entrenched tunnel will be used by the soldiers for safety.

Envy	**envy**	**envious**

I don't envy anybody.

I can see envy in your eyes.

Your envious nature is not good.

Equal	**equality**	**equal**

Sachin equalled Bradman's record long ago.

There should be equality between man and woman.

The equal share will be distributed.

Equivocate	**equivocation** **equivocal**	**equivocator**

The lawyer equivocated the case facts in the court.

The judge could see through the equivocation.

It was an equivocal argument.

Eradicate	**eradication** **eradicator**	**eradicable**

How can we eradicate malaria?

Eradication of polio is the prime objective of health department.

Eradicable diseases should be identified.

Erect	**erection** **erectness**	**erect**

The engineer will erect the machine.

The erection of the machine took full day.

The erect rod had to be bent to accommodate the machine.

Erode	**erosion**	**erosive**

Water will erode the metal from here.

We need to plant more trees to stop soil erosion.

The erosive chemical cannot be used in this process.

Err **error** **erroneous**

You erred in this matter.

There is a spelling error.

Avoid erroneous work.

Erupt **eruption** **eruptive**

The volcano will erupt anytime.

Many villages had to be evacuated because of volcanic eruption.

He has an eruptive temper.

Escort **escort** **escorted**

The policeman will escort the judge.

How many escorts will you need for the minister?

The escorted minister reached the place safely.

Establish **establishment** **established**

We can establish a good institute for training.

The establishment was envisioned by the great man.

It is difficult to compete with the established companies.

Esteem **esteem** **estimable**

I always esteemed that professor.

One should have high sense of self-esteem.

He has an estimable personality.

Estimate	**estimate** **estimation** **estimator**	**estimated**

How will they estimate the cost of the new building?
What is the estimate of the new building?
The estimated amount was not approved by the board of directors.

Eulogize	**eulogy**	**eulogistic**

He eulogized himself in the speech.
Self-eulogy is harmful.
Do you admire the eulogistic nature?

Evade	**evasion** **evasiveness evasive**	**evasively**

How did you evade the tax?
Tax evasion is not a good practice.
This evasive method will not yield the right result.

Evidence	**evidence**	**evident** **evidential**

Will you evidence in this case?
What is the evidence of the case?
The truth is evident.

Evoke	**evocation**	**evocative** **evocatively**

I will evoke the almighty to help us.
The evocation was done with a simple prayer.
The evocative speech was worth listening.

Evolve **evolution** **evolutionary**

This company evolved in time.
It is said that the evolution of man took many centuries.
The senior managers left the company in evolutionary time.

Exact **exaction** **exacting**

He exacted the budget with his experience.
How can we reach exaction in the project estimate?
The exacting figure did not match.

Exalt **exaltation** **exalted**

The students exalted themselves in the picnic.
He announced holiday for the staff in exaltation of the award.
The exalted people came into the field.

Exceed **excess** **excessive**

He will exceed the spending this time.
Remove the excess liquid from the drum.
The excessive baggage was removed from the plane.

Excel **excellence** **excellent**

He excels in software programming.
We should strive for excellence not perfection.
There is an excellent workshop in the town.

Except **exception** **exceptional**
exceptionable

All except Ramu went to the picnic.
Mahatma Gandhi was an exception among men.
Julius Caesar is an exceptional play.

Exchange	**exchange**	**exchangeable**

I will exchange this item.
What is the exchange rate of dollar?
The diamond is not exchangeable.

Excite	**excitement**	**excitable**
	excitability	**exciting**

The general excites spirit in the soldiers.
The excitement of the children was worthseeing.
It was an exciting match.

Exclaim	**exclamation**	**exclamatory**

He exclaimed at me.
The exclamation was seen on the face of the child.
Do not show your exclamatory expression to me.

Exclude	**exclusion**	**exclusive**
	exclusiveness	

Will you exclude him from the team?
Kapil's exclusion from the team was not good for this series.
It is an exclusive watch.

Exhaust	**exhaustion**	**exhausting**
		exhaustible

I have exhausted all money.
He sat out of exhaustion.
It was an exhausting walk.

Exhilarate	**exhilaration**	**exhilarating**
		exhilarated

We can exhilarate during the vacation.
They laughed out of exhilaration.
It was an exhilarating party.

Exist	**existence**	**existent**
		existential

He exists to eat only.
We should have a meaning of our existence.
There are many existential problems.

Expand	**expansion**	**expansive**
	expansiveness	**expansible**
		expandable

We need to expand our vision.
The expansion of the bridge will take one year.
The expansive farm was tilled by many workers.

Expect	**expectation**	**expectant**
	expectancy	

What do you expect from me?
Your expectation is high.
The expectant visitor could finally meet the manager.

Expel	**expulsion**	**expulsive**

We can expel him from the college.
The expulsion of the material will take sometime.
The expulsive procedure was explained by the scientist.

Experience	**experience**	**experienced** **experiential**

I experience happiness in talking to you.
What is your experience about this matter?
The experienced man was promoted.

Experiment	**experiment** **experimental**	**experimental**

We cannot experiment on humans.
The experiment should be done in laboratory only.
The experimental procedure is easy to understand.

Expire	**expiration**	**expiratory**

The old man expired last month.
Expiration of fathers is the history of mankind.
He took the expiratory breath.

Explain	**explanation**	**explanatory**

Please explain me this.
What is your explanation in this matter?
The explanatory statement seems incomplete.

Explode	**explosion** **explosiveness**	**explosive** **exploded**

The bomb exploded at night.
The explosion was very powerful.
It was an explosive statement.

Exploit	**exploitation** **exploiter**	**exploitative**

They exploited the labourers.
The exploitation of the poor is a sin.
His exploitative attitude will not approve the welfare activities.

Explore	**exploration** **explore**	**exploratory**

We explored the region.
The exploration of the area called for local help.
It is an exploratory activity.

Expose	**exposition**	**exposed**

You should expose the grains to sunlight.
The exposition of the items was not well planned.
The exposed wound was healed faster.

Express	**expression** **expressiveness**	**expressible** **expressive**

We should express it openly.
I like the expression on his face.
His expressive face told everything.

Extend	**extension** **extensiveness**	**extensive** **extensible**

Can we extend our leaves?
Kings wanted the extension of their kingdom.
The extensive work was given to our NGO.

Extract	**extraction**	**extractive**

Let us extract juice from this sugarcane.
The extraction of the juice calls for a machine.
What are the extractive elements in this chemical?

Extricate	**extrication**	**extricable**

How much juice can you extricate from a melon?
The extrication process is very long.
The extricable liquid is good.

Exult	**exultation**	**exultant**

We exulted in your company.
The boss declared a leave in exultation of the picnic.
The exultant mood is always good.

❑

F

VERB	NOUN	ADJECTIVE
Fail	**failure**	**failed**

I shall not fail in my mission.
Failures teach us a lot.
The failed student was counselled by the teacher.

Faint	**faintness**	**faint**

She fainted on seeing blood.
He took rest owing to faintness.
I have a faint memory of that neighbour.

Falsify	**falsification, falsity falseness**	**false**

Why should we falsify his statement?
There is falseness is his saying.
The false policeman was arrested.

Fancy	**fancy, fanciness**	**fanciful**

He fancied marrying her.
In my fancy I used to think of living on the hills.
The fanciful items are sold at high price.

Fascinate	**fascination**	**fascinating**

You fascinate me.
His fascination for her is great.
The fascinating painting was sold in the gallery.

Fathom	**fathom**	**fathomable** **fathomless**

I cannot fathom the intricacies of maths.
The fathom of the universe always attracts man.
The fathomable problem can be solved.

Favour	**favour**	**favourable** **favoured**

I did not favour anyone.
We thank God for his favour.
The ship will set in the sea in favourable weather.

Fear	**fear, fearfulness**	**fearsome** **fearful** **fearless**

We should not fear anyone.
Fear is a natural human factor.
The fearful deer did not come out of the bushes.

Feature	**feature**	**featureless**

He featured in the new film.
What is the feature of this machine?
The computer cannot be featureless.

Feel	**feeling**	**feeling**

Do you feel good now?
I understand your feelings.
Do you like her feeling nature?

Fetch	**fetching**	**fetchingly**

Will you fetch a glass for me?
The fetching sight is great.
She danced fetchingly.

Figure	**figure**	**figurative**

I figured that out.
Budget has a big figure.
It is a figurative drawing.
He spoke figuratively about life.

Fill	**filling**	**filling**

Please fill this form.
He wants filling of Rs. 1000.
The filling sensation seems to be over.

Film	**film**	**filmy**

The director filmed the famous novel.
Which film did you see recently?
Your filmy knowledge is good.

Finalise	**finalization** **finalist** **finality**	**final**

Let us finalize the date of the picnic.
The finalization of the budget took long time.
The final match was interesting.

Finger	**finger**	**fingerless**

Don't finger at me.
He has long fingers.
Have you seen a fingerless human?

Fire **fire** **fiery**

The soldiers fired at the terrorist.
The rangers are trying to control the forest fire.
His fiery eyes were red.

Firm **firmness** **firm**

He firmed his position in the company.
There was firmness in his voice.
The firm manager did not let the workers do as they please.

Fit **fit, fitness** **fit**

He fits in our company well.
You must walk daily for fitness.
The fit candidate was offered the job.

Fix **fix, fixation** **fixative, fixable**

Will you fix it?
He has fixation on the goal.
The fixable part should be repaired.

Flame **flame** **flammable**

The fire flames toward the south.
The flame was high.
Stay away from the flammable chemical.

Flatter **flatter, flattery** **flattering**

I flattered the child.
Be away from flattery.
Flattering is not a good habit.

Fleece	**fleece**	**fleecy**

The shrewd businessman fleeces his customers.
He lost many customers because of his fleece.
The fleecy attitude is not good in business.

Flirt	**flirtation** **flirtatiousness**	**flirtatious**

He does not flirt with anyone.
The flirtation proved to be bad for his reputation.
The flirtatious boy was sacked from the job.

Float	**float**	**floatable**

The wood floats on water.
The float of the boat was very smooth.
We have prepared a floatable box.

Flop	**flop, floppiness**	**floppy**

The film will flop.
The flop was due to the marketing strategy.
The floppy stature is not good to look at.

Flour	**flour**	**floury**

The food item is floured well.
I want flour of wheat.
There is a floury paste in the plate.

Flourish	**flourish**	**flourishing**

Good faith flourishes in this kingdom.
The flourish was due to the policies of the government.
The flourishing port was attacked by the pirates.

Flower	**flower**	**flowered**

The bush will flower soon.
It is a beautiful flower.
The flowered plant was the attraction of the festival.

Fluff	**fluff, fluffiness**	**fluffy**

The wind fluffed the plants.
The animals living in cold regions have fluffiness.
The fluffy dog was sitting on my lap.

Flush	**flush**	**flushed**

He flushed the chemical from the boiler.
The flush machine is not working.
The flushed waste can be recycled.

Foam	**foam**	**foamy**

The sea foamed due to high tide.
Children like to play with foam in tub.
That foamy material is a new chemical.

Focus	**focus**	**focal**

Did you focus on the problem?
What is the focus of your life?
The focal object is far from the microscope.

Follow	**follower, following**	**following**

I have followed my father's principles.
The followers of this religion do not believe in idol worship.
The following police team was called back.

Fool	**foolishness, fool**	**foolish**

You cannot fool me.
His foolishness is creating problems for others.
The foolish boy will be punished.

Force	**force** **forcefulness**	**forceful** **forcible**

The army forced the terrorists to surrender.
Use of force is neglected in democracy.
The CEO's forceful nature is sometimes not good.

Forget	**forgetfulness**	**forgetful** **forgettable**

I will not forget my grandparents.
Your forgetfulness will land you in trouble.
That forgetful worker left the machine running.

Forgive	**forgiveness**	**forgivable** **forgiving**

Will you forgive him?
Forgiveness calls for great moral courage.
It is not a forgivable crime.

Form	**form, formation**	**formative**

They formed a project team.
The formation of land took centuries.
The formative years of my career were filled with varied experience.

Formulate **formulation** **formulaic**

How did you formulate this idea?
The formulation of the chemical is flawless.
The formulaic catalyst has to be added in it.

Forward **forward** **forward**

He forwarded the mail to me.
The forward of the building has a wonderful view.
The forward thought in this philosophy is worth reading.

Foul **foulness** **foul**

They fouled the place while working.
The smell is due to foulness.
The foul smell comes from that corner.

Fox **foxiness** **foxed**
fox like, foxy

He foxed us in the deal.
His foxiness will not go for long.
The foxy attitude of my brother needs to be controlled.

Free **free, freedom** **free**

The court freed him.
India got freedom in 1947.
The free man can think about the solutions to problems.

Frequent **frequency** **frequent**

A tiger frequents this river.
The train has a good frequency.
The frequent traveller was given discount.

Fret	**fret**	**fretful**

The mother frets for the son.
He seems old because of the fret in his mind.
The fretful problem brought loss to the company.

Frighten	**fright**	**frightful** **frightening**

Why do you frighten the kids?
The child cried in fright.
It was frightful sight.

Frisk	**frisk, friskiness**	**frisky**

The kids are frisking in the garden.
They enjoyed the frisk with music.
The frisky mood lasted long.

Frolic	**frolic**	**frolicsome**

Why are they frolicking?
The frolic was great at the party.
The frolicsome couple enjoyed each other's company.

Front	**front, frontage**	**frontal**

The commander will front the mission.
Do not park in the front.
The frontal gate is closed.

Frost	**frost, frostiness**	**frosty**

It will frost in winter.
The frost is tremendous this time.
The frosty weather looked good.

Frustrate	**frustration**	**frustrate** **frustrating** **frustratingly**

The boss frustrated them.
He shouted in frustration.
The frustrated man committed suicide.

Fry	**fry**	**fried**

I will fry some wafers for you.
Fry takes much oil.
The fried vegetables are put on the table.

Fulfil	**fulfilment**	**fulfilled**

How can you fulfil your dreams?
Fulfilment of dreams calls for hard work.
The fulfilled dream should be cherished.

Function	**function**	**functional**

He functions as ticket collector in railways.
There is a function in the honour of the new minister.
The students are trained in functional English.

Fur	**fur**	**furred**

The lambs furred when they were two.
The fur is good for making warm cloths.
The furred coat can be used in winter.

Further	**furtherance**	**further**

How should we further the process?
The furtherance of business requires aggressiveness.
The further road is better.

Fuse	**fuse, fusibility fusion**	**fusible**

The goats fused with sheep.
There is fusion of music in the modern times.
The fusible music was well composed.

Fuss	**fuss, fussiness**	**fussy**

I have not fussed over the matter.
His fussiness is not good.
The fussy teacher was asked to leave the school.

❑

G

VERB	NOUN	ADJECTIVE
Gain	**gain**	**gainful**

He has gained weight.
The gain was good in this deal.
The gainful business cannot be closed.

Galvanize	**galvanization**	**galvanized**

Let us galvanize the machine.
The galvanization process is costly.
The galvanized cupboard looked new.

Generate	**generation** **generator**	**generative**

The plant will generate electricity.
Generation of wealth is not easy.
The generative power plant was closed down.

Germinate	**germination**	**germinative**

The seeds germinated well.
Germination is not possible without water.
Germinative process is described in the book of biology.

Giggle	**giggle**	**giggly**

Do not giggle in the class.
The giggle was loud and clear.
The giggly boy was asked to leave the class.

Glare	**glare**	**glaring**

I glared at the animal.
There was glare coming from the south side.
The glaring mistake cannot be improved.

Glitter	**glitter**	**glittery**

Gold glitters everywhere.
The glitter of the diamond is very attractive.
The glittery stone is not diamond.

Glorify	**glory, glorification**	**glorious**

They glorified the king.
Many poems were written in the king's glorification.
The glorious palace was built 200 years ago.

Glow	**glow**	**glowing**

The insect glowed at night.
The glow of the fire was seen from far.
The glowing stone was taken out of the mine.

Glue	**glue**	**gluey**

He glued to the seat for hours.
The effect of the glue was great.
The gluey paste was washed with water.

Glut	**gluttony**	**glutton** **gluttonous**

He gluts food thrice a day.
Gluttony is not good.
The gluttonous boy fell ill.

Gossip	**gossip**	**gossipy**

Do not gossip in the office.
The gossip was controlled by the management.
The gossipy employee was punished.

Govern	**government** **governance**	**governmental**

The king governs well.
The government has to work for the welfare of the people.
There are some governmental problems in democracy.

Grace	**grace** **gracefulness**	**graceful** **graceless**

The judge graced the occasion.
Look at her grace!
The graceful heroine enthralled everyone.

Grade	**grade, gradation**	**gradational**

How did you grade the products?
The gradational criteria will be decided soon.

Gratify	**gratification**	**grateful**

The tasty food gratified his hunger.
Lot of food is required for the gratification of elephant.
The grateful thank everyone.

Gravitate	**gravitation**	**gravitational**

The ball gravitated lightly.
All objects fall owing to gravitation.
The gravitational force is supreme on the earth.

Grieve	**grief**	**grievous**

Why do you grieve for him?
The grief of the loss of dear ones is great.
The grievous family was comforted by the neighbours.

Grub	**grubbiness**	**grubby**

The animal grubbed the ground.
The grubbiness cannot be cleaned easily.
The grubby floor need water treatment for cleaning.

Guard	**guard**	**guarded**

The dog guards the house well.
The guard stands at the gate.
The guarded fort cannot be looted easily.

Guide	**guide, guidance**	**guiding**

He guides his students well.
Your guidance in the technical subject is solicited.
Honesty is the guiding principle of my life.

Gum	**gum**	**gummy**

The papers gummed together.
Put some gum on the cardboard.
The gummy substance did not stick properly.

Gust	**gust**	**gusty**

The wind gusted in.
The gust was so powerful that the window panes were broken.
The gusty wind blew away the tent.

Gyrate	**gyration**	**gyratory**

The planets gyrated around the sun.
The gyration of the belt is slow.
The gyratory movement is not smooth.

❑

H

VERB	NOUN	ADJECTIVE
Habituate	**habituation** **habit**	**habitual**

I habituated my son to wake up early.
It is not good habit to smoke.
The habitual movement of the hand has to be controlled.

Hack	**hack, hacking**	**hacked**

The farmer hacked the wood.
It was not an easy hack for the woodcutter.
The hacked site could not be restored.

Hallucinate	**hallucination**	**hallucinatory**

The poet hallucinated of the old times.
He woke up on seeing hallucination.
The hallucinatory condition of the mind is sometimes not good.

Heat	**heat**	**heated, hot**

The metal heats up fast.
The heat is tremendous in summer.
The heated bread can be cut easily.

Heed	**heedful, heedless**	**heedlessly**

Do not heed to his words.
The heedful man has less to fear.
He worked heedlessly and met with an accident.

Help	**help, helpfulness**	**helpful**

Did you help him?
Your help is needed here.
The helpful teacher is always popular.

Herald	**herald, heraldry**	**heraldic**

The cock heralds the dawn.
Do not neglect a good herald.
It is a heraldic sign of a revolution.

Hesitate	**hesitation, hesitance**	**hesitant**

He does not hesitate to speak in front of many people.
The hesitation is due to lack of practice.
The hesitant guest was given food and water.

Hire	**hire, hirer**	**hireable**

We hired some officers in our bank.
The company's hire was fast this time.
Is he a hireable candidate?

Hollow	**hollowness**	**hollow**

The wind hollowed the stone cave.
Some animals live in the hollowness of the mountain.
The hollow wood is not strong.

Honour	**honour**	**honourable** **honorary** **honourably**

I honour all women.
It was an honour to live in the times of Mahatma Gandhi.
The honorary lecture was delivered by the chief guest.

Hope	**hope** **hopelessness**	**hopeful** **hopeless**

I hope to get first rank this time.
Is there hope of victory this time?
The hopeless boy was finally removed from the class.

Horrify	**horror**	**horrible** **horrifying** **horrific**

Did the movie horrify you?
I could see the horror in his eyes.
The horrible night will never be forgotten.

Humiliate	**humiliation**	**humiliating**

Why did you humiliate him?
Humiliation did not disturb him.
After the humiliating experience he left the job.

Hunger **hunger** **hungry**

She hungers to see the parents.
Hunger knows no race or creed.
The hungry tiger set out to hunt.

Hunt **hunt, hunter, hunting** **hunted**

The tiger hunts for food.
The hunter hid behind the tree.
The hunted deer was taken by the lion.

❑

I

VERB	NOUN	ADJECTIVE
Ice	**icing, ice**	**icy**

The bartender iced the drink for me.
There is lot of ice in the refrigerator.
He has icy expressions.

Identify	**identification**	**identifiable**

Did he identify the criminal?

The identification of the criminal was done in the police station.

It is not an identifiable problem.

Idle	**idleness, idler**	**idle**

The children idle during vacation.
He missed the project in idleness.
That idle boy should be trained strictly.

Ignore	**ignorance**	**ignorant**

Why did he ignore you?
Ignorance is not good.
The ignorant people were exploited by the politician.

Illuminate	**illumination**	**illuminating** **illuminative**

Ramu will illuminate the building.
The illumination of the city is the task of the municipality.
The illuminative personalities were present at the function.

Illustrate	**illustration** **illustrator**	**illustrative**

We should illustrate the matter properly in the text book.
There is an illustration of this problem.
His illustrative boy makes him proud.

Imagine	**imagination** **imaginativeness**	**imaginary** **imaginative**

I imagined about the upcoming vacation.
Poets must have great imagination.
The imaginary world was depicted in the novel.

Imitate	**imitator** **imitation**	**imitable** **imitative**

Do not imitate everyone like a monkey.
It is imitation jewellery.
The imitative nature will not develop your own personality.

Immigrate	**immigration** **immigrant**	**immigrant**

When did they immigrate to UK?
The immigration agent helped us a lot.
The immigrants are treated as secondary citizens in this country.

Impact	**impact, impaction**	**impacted**

Gandhiji impacted a lot the thought of the world.
The impact of the blast was seen till a long distance.
The impacted city was evacuated.

Impeach	**impeachment**	**impeachable**

I impeach him in the name of humanity.
The impeachment of Warren Hastings was a historical case.
All citizens are impeachable if they commit crime.

Imply	**implication**	**implicit**

The advice of the saint implies to all of us.
What are the implications of this law?
He is implicit motive is not good.

Impose	**imposition**	**imposing**

Please impose some restrictions on them.
The imposition of the rules is not easy.
His imposing personality was respected everywhere.

Impress	**impression** **impressiveness**	**impressive**

You impressed me by your performance.
What is your impression about him?
His impressive dress is very costly.

Improve	**improvement**	**improvable**

How can I improve my language?
Improvement in the system is required urgently.
Your speech is improvable.

Improvise	**improvisation**	**improvisational** **improvisatory**

He may improvise the new design.
A meeting was held for improvisation of the structural design of the building.
The improvisational bill was passed in the parliament.

Inaugurate	**inauguration** **inaugurator**	**inaugural**

The minister will inaugurate the new plant.
How many guests were present at the inauguration ceremony?
The Chairman delivered the inaugural speech.

Include	**inclusion** **inclusiveness**	**inclusive**

What will you include in this list?
The inclusion of Hari in the team is a good decision.
The inclusive taxes are not much.

Incorporate	**incorporation**	**incorporated**

We can incorporate this policy from the next year.
The incorporation of the policy will take time.
The incorporated tax amendment will be read out in the assembly.

Increase	**increase**	**increasingly**

Please increase your working hours.
There is slight increase in the child's weight.
He earns increasingly.

Incriminate	incrimination	incriminatory

The police are incriminating the burglar.
The incrimination procedure was followed by the court.
The plaintiff read out the incriminatory statement in the court.

Indicate	indication indicator	indicative indicatory

I indicated him as friend.
The manager's indication towards the project is worth thinking.
Your indicative remarks will not be understood.

Indict	indictment	indictable

We indict him under three provisions of Indian Penal Code.
The indictment of the politician was not an easy job.
It is an indictable crime.

Indulge	indulgence	indulgent

Do not indulge in gossip.
Self-indulgence is not always good.
Beware of his indulgent nature.

Industrialize	industrialization industry	industrial

The government needs to industrialize this area.
Manufacturing industry is booming in India.
There is good industrial growth.

Infect	infection	infectious

How will the disease infect the children?
There is severe infection of the throat.
It is an infectious disease.

Infer	**inference**	**inferable** **inferential**

What did you infer from his statement?
The inference of the police officer was right.
The inferential statement was produced before the court.

Inflame	**inflammation**	**inflammable** **inflammatory**

Their behaviour inflamed the father.
Apply this cream on the inflammation of the skin.
This is an inflammable chemical.

Inflect	**inflection**	**inflective**

The leader inflected many times during the speech.
You need to work on your inflection.
It was an inflective pause.

Influence	**influence**	**influential**

His teacher influenced his thoughts.
We can see the influence of Mughal culture in many cities.
The influential tycoon managed to get the contract.

Inform	**information** **informer**	**informative**

Did you inform him that you are not coming?
What is the information about the position of the army?
You should read the informative article in the class.

Ingratiate	**ingratiating**	**ingratiatingly**

I will ingratiate for him.
My ingratiating friend came to me.
He talked ingratiatingly before the election to the voters.

Inhabit	**inhabitant**	**inhabitable**

Many animals inhabit in this forest.
Lion is the inhabitant of Gir.
It is an inhabitable place for humans.

Inherit	**inheritance** **inheritor**	**inheritable**

He will inherit the property of his father.
What is the amount of inheritance?
It is an inheritable disease.

Inhibit	**inhibition**	**inhibited**

The striking workers inhibit the speed of the production.
Is there any inhibition in anyone's mind about this project?
The inhibited team could not perform well.

Injure	**injury**	**injured, injurious**

Who injured this poor deer?
There is slight injury on his left leg.
The injured batsman retired to the pavilion.

Ink	**ink, inkiness**	**inky**

The peon inked the parcel.
Do not spill the ink on the table.
I will not wear this inky shirt.

Inscribe	**inscription**	**inscriptional**

What is inscribed on the tree?
There is some inscription on the ancient rock.
The ancient inscriptional scrip was deciphered by the historian.

Insist	**insistence**	**insistent**

He insists on coming with us.

Parents left the plan of going our because of the insistence of the children.

The insistent child was taken along by the father.

Inspire	**inspiration**	**inspire** **inspiring**

Who inspired you to such a noble work?

One needs inspiration to be a great artist.

We clapped on hearing the inspiring speech.

Institute	**institution**	**institutional**

The leader instituted certain doctrines of humanity.

He works in a government institution.

The institutional funding will not be enough for this project.

Instruct	**instruction** **instructor**	**instructional** **instructive**

Please instruct the cadets.

The instructor of computer lab was a learned man.

First read the instructive points and then begin the work.

Insult	**insult**	**insulting**

We shall not insult him.

He did not heed the insult and continued his work.

Take back your insulting remark.

Insure	**insurer, insurance**	**insured**

I have to insure myself with a big sum.

What are the terms of this insurance?

The insured sum was huge.

Intensify	**intensification** **intensity**	**intensive**

The cold in our city intensified as there was snowfall in the Himalayas.

The intensity of reading is more important.

Labour intensive industries cannot be managed easily.

Interact	**interaction**	**interactive**

My students interact in the class.

What did you learn from the interaction?

There will be interactive session after lunch.

Interchange	**interchange**	**interchangeable**

Ram and Shyam interchanged the seats.

Interchange of property requires lot of paper work.

These parts of the machine are not interchangeable.

Interest	**interest**	**interesting**

Are you interested in joining us for a movie?

The interest rate has increased.

Please read out that interesting story to the children.

Interpret	**interpretation** **interpreter**	**interpretative** **interpretive**

Do not interpret meaning of this sentence.

What was the interpretation after studying a case?

The scientist's interpretive comments are good.

Intrigue	**intrigue**	**intriguing**

The kings intrigued against each other in old times.

The intrigue to topple the government was unearthed.

The intriguing kings were attacked by a foreign power and defeated.

Introduce	**introduction**	**introductory** **introducible**

Please introduce him to me.

The introduction of the guest was given loudly.

The CEO's introductory speech was motivating.

Intrude	**intrusion, intruder**	**intrusive**

I don't intrude in other people's privacy.

Please ignore such intrusions.

The intrusive boy was asked to leave the class.

Invade	**invasion, invader**	**invasive**

Many foreign rulers invaded India.

The invasion of Alexander was in the time of Chanakya.

The invasive army was defeated.

Invent	**invention, inventor**	**inventive**

Who invented the TV?

Invention of computer revolutionized the world.

It was an inventive experiment.

Investigate	**investigation** **investigator**	**investigative** **investigatory**

The police department will investigate the fraud.

Investigation was carried out by expert officers of the police.

I would like to give this matter to an investigative agency.

Invite	**invitation**	**inviting**

Who invited them for dinner?
Have you received my invitation card?
The inviting cake was placed on the table.

Invoke	**invocation**	**invocatory**

Let us invoke God to help us.
The epic begins with an invocation.
The invocatory pages were read before the audience.

Irk		**irksome**

Don't irk the child.
The irksome kid was not welcomed anywhere.

Irrigate	**irrigation** **irrigator**	**irrigable**

Did the farmer irrigate the field in morning?
The canal was built for irrigation purpose.
It is not an irrigable land.

Irritate	**irritation**	**irritable**

He irritates me every time.
There is irritation on the skin.
Bad health has made her nature irritable.

Itch	**itch, itchiness**	**itchy**

The boil on the skin itches a lot.
Apply this cream to get rid of itchiness.
The itchy skin became red.

❑

J

VERB	NOUN	ADJECTIVE
Jeer	**jeered**	

The children jeered the monkeys.
Their jeer was not liked by me.

Jerk	**jerk, jerkiness**	**jerky**

He will not jerk the car.
The jerk was very powerful.
His jerky movements have to be improved.

Joke	**joke, joker**	**jokey**

Do not joke in class.
The joker was employed in the circus.
The jokey man became popular.

Judge	**judgement, judge**	**judgemental**

Do not judge anyone on the face value.
Your judgement about this company was right.
The judgemental statement was clear.

Justify	**justice** **justification**	**justificatory**

How will you justify this act?
Justice delayed is justice denied.
The justificatory act was hailed by the people.

❑

K

VERB	NOUN	ADJECTIVE
Knot	**knot**	**knotty**

I cannot knot this string.
The knot is tough to untie.
The knotty problem was solved.

VERB	NOUN	ADJECTIVE
Know	**knowledge**	**knowing**

Your knowledge about fish is good.

The knowledgeable professor was given an important assignment.

❑

L

VERB	NOUN	ADJECTIVE
Labour	**labour, labourer**	**laboured** **laborious**

He laboured for many days to complete the work.
How many labourers work in your factory?
The laborious task was given to the new workers.

Lack	**lack**	**lacking**

The painting lacks emotions.
Is there lack of money in this business?
The lacking business was given a breather with new loan.

Lament	**lamentation**	**lamented** **lamentable**

Why lament on it now?
He was upset owing to lamentation.
It was a lamentable loss to us.

Languish	**languor**	**languorous**
		languid

He languished after the disease.
He sat down owing to languor.
Avoid delivering this languid speech.

Lapse	**lapse**	**lapsed**

You lapsed at one point in the speech.
We lost the project bid because of a lapse in design.
The lapsed item cannot be sold.

Laud	**laud**	**laudable**
	laudability	**laudatory**

The audience lauded his performance.
He was happy because of the laud of the public.
The victorious captain was showered with laudatory comments.

Laugh	**laugh, laughter**	**laughable**
	laughing	

Don't laugh in the class.
The laughter was very loud.
It is not a laughable joke.

Lavish	**lavish**	**lavishly**

The young man has always lavished because of his rich father.
The lavish party was organized at the Taj Hotel.
He spent lavishly on his girlfriend.

Laze **laziness** **lazy**

The animal lazed around in summer.

Laziness is enemy of ambition.

The lazy dog did not get much to eat.

Lead **leadership, leader** **leading**

I lead the team of my city.

India won freedom under the leadership of Mahatma Gandhi.

The leading industrialists were invited by the Prime Minister to discuss.

Leak **leakage** **leaky**

He leaked the news to police.

There is leakage in the new canal which has to be repaired soon.

The leaky roof will be repaired before monsoon.

Learn **learning, learner** **learned**

What did you learn today in school?

He is a fast learner.

The learned advocates present the case.

Liberate **liberty, liberation, liberator** **liberate**

Great leaders liberated our country from the British rule.

India got liberty in 1947.

The liberate mind can think many things.

Light	**light**	**light**

Sun lights the world.
The food is light, patient can eat it.
The light vehicle can only cross the bridge.

Like	**liking**	**likeable**

He likes my car.
There is liking between them.
It is a likeable child.

Limit	**limit, limitation**	**limited limitless**

Do not limit yourself here.
What is your limitation in going ahead?
The limitless universe has many mysteries.

Line	**line, linearity**	**linear**

People lined up to worship at temple.
There is a big line at the theatre.
The linear motion of the car is due to some mechanism.

Live	**life**	**liveable, live**

Many animals live in this forest.
Life is very precious.
It is not a liveable place.

Load	**load, loader**	**loaded, loading**

They loaded the truck with goods.
We need to remove some load from the truck to make it move well.
The loaded truck tumbled near the bridge.

Loft	**loftiness**	**lofty**

The engineer lofted the model of the plane.
He spoke with loftiness about himself.
The lofty shot was hit by the captain.

Loosen	**looseness**	**loose**

Loosen the reins of the horse.
Looseness of character is not good.
The loose poster fell on the ground.

Love	**love, lover**	**loveable**

He loves you very much.
Love is a great feeling and experience.
She is a lovable child.

Lower	**low, lowness** **lowliness**	**lowly**

He lowered the boat into the sea from ship.
Such a thought shows lowliness in his character.
His lowly character repels him from everywhere.

❑

M

VERB	NOUN	ADJECTIVE
Madden	**madness**	**mad, maddening**

The chaos in the house maddened the home maker.
There was madness during the participation of India.
The mad man was sent to the hospital for treatment.

Magnetize	**magnet** **magnetization**	**magnetic**

The hills always magnetize me for a vacation.
There is a magnet in this machine.
His magnetic personality drew the mass towards him.

Magnify	**magnification** **magnifier**	**magnetisable**

Do not magnify this problem.

The magnification of the grain will help you to understand it better.

Is this metal magnetisable?

Malign	**malignity** **malignancy**	**malignant**

He maligned our reputation in the society.
The malignity among religions is not good in the society.
The malignant intention of the religious leaders was understood by the people.

Manage	**management** **manager**	**manageable** **managerial**

How do you manage house and office together?
The manager has the authority to approve this bill.
The event is manageable.

Manifest	**manifestation**	**manifest**

I would like to manifest my skills in the function.

The Dandi March was a manifestation of unity of the people of India.

The manifest strength of military is real to the core.

Manipulate	**manipulation** **manipulator**	**manipulative**

Do not try to manipulate the facts.

Manipulation of facts and statements is a routine with lawyers.

The manipulative tactics of the lawyer did not work in front of the judge.

Mark	**mark**	**marked**

I marked him absent in the class.
He has got good marks in the exam.
The marked difference can be seen between the twins.

Market	**market, marketing** **marketer** **marketability**	**marketable**

How will the company market its new product with minimum budget?

You will find many competitors in the market.

It is not a marketable product.

Marvel	**marvel**	**marvellous**

The child marvelled at the design.

Taj Mahal is a marvel.

What a marvellous building!

Master	**master**	**masterful** **masterly**

You should master the art of making speeches.

Bruce Lee was a master of martial arts.

Your masterful behaviour is not liked by your friends.

Mature	**maturation**	**mature** **maturity**

The child is maturing gradually.

He could take this decision because of his maturity.

The mature man was selected for a responsible position.

Measure	**measurement**	**measureless**

Let us measure the length of this room.

What is the measurement of the ground?

Sky is measureless.

Migrate **migration** **migratory**

The birds migrate to India every winter.

A lot of migration took place owing to war in the Middle East.

We went to the sanctuary to see migratory birds.

Mimic **mimicry** **mimetic**

I mimicked the great actor in the programme.

Mimicry is an art that needs observation and practice.

The mimetic boy was punished by the principal in the school.

Mind **mind** **mindful**

I won't mind his presence here.

Do what your mind says.

The mindful workers can avoid accidents in the factory.

Minimize **minimization** **minimum**

How can we minimize risk in this plant?

Minimization of risk in the plants calls for upgrading the technology and discarding old machines.

We gave minimun estimate to them.

Minister **minister** **ministerial**

He ministers the poor.

Who became the finance minister?

We were into the ministerial services.

Mistake **mistake** **mistaken**

You have mistaken in judging him.

Your mistake will prove dangerous.

It is a case of mistaken identity.

Mock **mockery, mocker** **mock**

His friends mocked him in the class.
Do not do mockery of the law.
Mock practice should be done regularly.

Moisten **moisture** **moist**

Moisten this piece of cloth.
There is still moisture in the flour.
I will not wear moist cloth.

Monopolize **monopoly, monopolization** **monopolistic**

Government monopolized the supply of sugar and salt.
He enjoys monopoly in his house.
The monopolistic policies of government are not good for the people in the long run.

Mortgage **mortgage, mortgager** **mortgageable**

I would like to mortgage this property.
What is the procedure of mortgage in bank?
Bank will accept only mortgageable property.

Mortify **mortification** **mortifying**

He mortified everyone present with his words.
Mortification of the parents is due to the son's behaviour.
It was a mortifying behaviour.

Mother **motherhood** **motherly**
motherliness

She mothered two sons.
Motherhood is desired by for all women.
The motherly care of the warden was missed by the girls.

Motivate **motivation** **motivational**

Will you motivate them to accomplish the mission?
He has tremendous motivation to do the work.
We want to organize a motivational programme.

Mourn **mourner, mourning** **mournful**

She mourns the death of her father still.
The mourning after the death of the head of family lasted long.
30th January, 1948 was a mournful day for India.

Move **movement, mover** **moveable**

Ram will move from here.
We are observing the movement of animals in this forest.
It is not a moveable cupboard.

Muck **muck** **mucky**

The flood mucked the whole city.
We had to clean the muck from the area.
The mucky land had to be treated for long.

Muffle **muffler** **muffled**

The roar of the lion muffled the tourists.
I have a muffler to protect from cold.
The muffled tourists waited for the lion to pass from there.

Murder	**murder, murderer**	**murderous**

The gangster murdered his enemy.
There was trial for murder in the High Court.
His murderous attack was repelled by me.

Mutiny	**mutiny, mutineer**	**mutinous**

The soldiers mutinied against the British Raj in 1857.
What was the cause of the mutiny in 1857?
He came to the room in a mutinous mood.

Mystify	**mystification** **mystery**	**mystical**

He is mystifying the facts.
There is no mystery in the matter now.
The mystical man was then not seen anywhere.

❑

N

VERB	NOUN	ADJECTIVE
Name	**name**	**nameable** **nameless**

Please name a few good places to visit in India.
What is your name?
The nameless baby was adopted by a couple.

Narrate	**narration** **narrator**	**narrative**

He narrated his experience of war.
The narration in the novel is well done.
The narrative paragraph can be read aloud in the class.

Narrow	**narrowness**	**narrow**

The municipality did not narrow the roads.
The narrowness of mind is an obstacle to progress.
The narrow lane is dark and dinghy.

Nationalize	**nationalization**	**national**
	nation	

The government nationalized many banks.
Ours is a great nation.
The national holidays are observed by companies.

Navigate	**navigation**	**navigational**
	navigator	**navigable**
	navigability	

The ship will navigate through the canal early in the morning.
An expert navigator knows when to put up the sails.
Is it a navigable canal?

Near	**nearness**	**near**

The enemy is nearing the fort?
Nearness to eyes ensures nearness to heart.
The nearones of the old man were called by the doctor.

Need	**need**	**needful**
	necessity	**necessary, needy**

Do you need the papers now?
There is a necessity of good governance.
The needy people were helped by the NGO.

Negate	**negation,**	**negative**
	negativity	

Can you negate this point?
There is no negativity about you in my mind.
The negative mindset is not good.

Neglect	**negligence**	**neglectful** **negligent**

He neglects his health very much.
There is no reason of negligence in this work.
The negligent workers were sent to training of safety.

Negotiate	**negotiation**	**negotiator**

Shall we negotiate with them?
The negotiation took place between the directors of the two companies.
You are an excellent negotiator.

Neutralize	**neutralization** **neutrality**	**neutral**

This medicine will neutralize the effect of infection.
He kept quiet in the meeting to show neutralization.
The neutral manager was sought after for advice.

Nominate	**nomination** **nominator** **nominee**	**nominated**

Whom will you nominate for the post?
The nomination papers were filed before the election.
The nominated candidate got lot of support.

Notice	**notice**	**noticeable**

Did you notice his behaviour in the meeting?
There is a notice at the entrance of the theatre about pick-pockets.
It is a noticeable change in him.

Notify **notification** **notifiable**

How will you notify them?
Is there a notification in the magazine?
Polio is a notifiable disease.

Nourish **nourishment** **nourishing**

He should nourish the children well.
This food is tasty but lacks in nourishment.
The nourishing food may not taste well always.

Numb **numbness** **numb**

Cold numbs the fingers.
He could not move the fingers well because of numbness.
The numb hand was treated by the doctor.

Number **number** **numberless**

I have numbered the pages of the thesis.
Three is my lucky number.
The numberless cars were detained by the police.

❑

O

VERB	NOUN	ADJECTIVE
Obey	**obedience**	**obedient**

We should obey the traffic rules.
He stood up in obedience of the judge.
An obedient son is well cultured.

VERB	NOUN	ADJECTIVE
Object	**objection** **objector**	**objectionable**

I object to his behaviour.
What was the objection of the manager in this budget?
It is an objectionable point.

VERB	NOUN	ADJECTIVE
Oblige	**obligation**	**obliged** **obligatory** **obliging**

Please oblige us by sending the payment.
How can I repay your obligation?
It is an obligatory duty of the children to look after parents in their old age.

Obscure	**obscurity**	**obscure**

Why do you obscure the topic to the students?
There is no obscurity in this matter.
Please explain again this obscure topic.

Observe	**observation** **observer**	**observant** **observational** **observable**

What did you observe in this experiment?
The observation of the old labourer is right.
The enemy movement was caught by the observant sentry at the border.

Obstruct	**obstruction**	**obstructive**

Do not obstruct this road.
There is obstruction at the corner of the road.
We have to overcome all the obstructive forces.

Oil	**oil, oiliness**	**oily**

The mechanic is oiling the parts of the car.
Oil is a very valuable commodity today.
His hair is oily and needs washing.

Open	**openness**	**open**

The servant opened the door for us.
Let us move out in openness to get fresh air.
The open gate should be shut at night.

Operate	**operation**	**operational**
	operator	**operative**

The doctor operated the patient.
The operation of a BPO is not easy and is at odd time.
There are some operational problems in the company.

Oppose	**opposition, oppose**	**opposite**

Why did he oppose me?

The opposition party is questioning the government on this law.

The opposite house is owned by my uncle.

Oppress	**oppression**	**oppressive**
	oppressor	
	oppressiveness	

We shall oppress the revolt with a heavy hand.
People should not cow down to the oppressor.
The oppressive government is not accepted for a long time.

Opt	**option**	**optional**

What did you opt for?
I will go for the second option.
Accounts is an optional paper.

Organize	**organization, organizer**	**organizational**

Let us organize a workshop in the institute.
Which organization is the best in service?
This is our organizational goal.

Orient	**orientation**	**oriental**

Let us orient the new employees with the process.
I went to attend an orientation programme at the academy.
We have some oriental delicacies in our menu.

Originate	**originator** **origination**	**original**

From where does *Ganga* originate?
What is the origination of the literature?
The original copy was sold at high price.

❑

P

VERB	NOUN	ADJECTIVE
Pacify	**pacification**	**pacificatory**

How will you pacify the child?
I used to be given a chocolate by parents in pacification.
It was a pacificatory gift for the child.

VERB	NOUN	ADJECTIVE
Pain	**pain**	**painful** **painless** **pained**

The injury pains a lot.
The child cried in pain.
The painful limb was bandaged by the doctor.
The citizens spoke painfully of the war.

VERB	NOUN	ADJECTIVE
Pale	**paleness**	**pale**

Sickness has paled you face.
There is paleness on your face.
The wall looks pale in this building.

Panic **panic** **panicky**

He panics fast, which is not a good quality in a manager.
The people ran in panic.
The panicky boy was pacified by the parents.

Parallel **parallelism** **parallel**

He parallels his father in business skills.
How do you establish parallelism between literature and management?
Draw two parallel lines on this board.

Paralyse **paralysis** **paralytic**

The strike paralyzed the movement of the city.
He is being treated for paralysis.
It was a paralytic.

Pardon **pardon** **pardonable**
parody parodist

I pardon him for this mistake.
Who pronounced the pardon to them?
It is not a pardonable crime.

Participate **participation** **participatory**
participator
participant

Will you participate in the race?
How many participants are there in the elocution competition?
The participatory form will be filled.

Pass	**passage, passer**	**passable**

He passed the exam with good marks.
The wound will heal with passage of time.
Make only passable jokes.

Patch	**patch, patchiness**	**patchy**

The mason patched the leaking roof.
The patch of the road is quite long.
It is a patchy roof.

Patronize	**patronage, patron**	**patronizing**

I patronize his performance.
All artists need patrons of art.
It was a patronizing gesture by the leader.

Pay	**payment**	**paid**
	payee	**payable**

How much did he pay you?
The payment was done in cheque.
What is the payable amount?

Peeve	**peeve**	**peevish**
		peeve

I am not peeved by his remark.
He spoke like that because of the peeve.
His peevish voice did not stir anyone.

Penetrate	**penetration, penetrability**	**penetrable penetrative penetrating**

The sun rays penetrated the woods.

The penetration of Gandhi's thoughts was because of his practice.

The penetrating nail cannot be blunt.

Pension	**pensioner**	**pensionable**

The king pensions many old ministers.

How many pensioners are there in you club?

The modern jobs are not pensionable.

People	**people**	**people**

The new civilization gradually peopled.

How many people were there in the meeting?

It was a people movement.

Perceive	**perception perceptibility**	**perceivable perceptible**

I have perceived the matter well.

What is your perception about this case?

The perceivable problem was discussed in the board meeting.

Perfect	**perfection perfectibility**	**perfectible**

I have perfected the art of paper cutting.

Why do you try for perfection always?

Human mind is not perfectible.

Perjure	**perjury, perjurer**	**perjured**

He perjured in the court.
The trial is for perjury.
The perjured statement was recorded by the judge.

Permeate	**permeation**	**permeable**
	permeability	

Liquid permeates from this.
Is there permeability in this material?
The permeable part of the machine has to be repaired.

Permit	**permission**	**permissible**
	permissibility	**permissive**

I cannot permit this work here.
You must take permission before coming.
It should be done in permissible limits of the society.

Persist	**persistence**	**persistent**

The cold and cough still persists.
I came here because of the persistence of my friend.
The persistent engineer invented the machine.

Persuade	**persuasion**	**persuadable**
	persuasiveness	**perusable**
	persuasive	

What will you persuade after your graduation?
Your persuasion does not work with me.
Is it a perusable goal?

Pervade	**pervasion**	**pervasive**

Sunlight pervades through the screen.
The water reduced from the pot owing to pervasion.
It is a pervasive statement.

Pervert	**perversion**	**perverted**

This incident perverted his mind a lot.
He does such things because of perversion.
The perverted person is not a good company.

Photograph	**photograph** **photography** **photographer**	**photographic**

He photographs skilfully.
Photography is a science as well as an art.
You have a photographic eye.

Picture	**picture**	**pictorial**

I pictured the scene in my mind.
It is a beautiful picture.
What a pictorial design!

Pinch	**pinch**	**pinched**

Do not pinch the child, it will hurt.
Your pinch is very sharp.
His pinched ego angered him.

Pirate	**piracy**	**piratical**

They pirated some movies.
Piracy act is enforced by the government.
It is a piratical process of the software.

Pit	**pit**	**pitted**

The manager will pit us against each other.
The animal has fallen in a pit.
They ran into a pitted ground.

Pity	**pity**	**pitying**

I pitied the poor old beggar.
Take pity on the handicap people.
The pitying heart is blessed.

Pivot	**pivot**	**pivotal**

My life pivots around you.
What is the pivot of this wheel?
It was a pivotal point of my career.

Place	**placement**	**placed**

We placed him in a good company.
There is a placement cell in our institute.
Well placed people too have many enemies.

Plan	**plan, planning planner**	**planned**

I am planning a vacation.
Planning must be done well in advance.
How was your planned event?

Plant	**plantation**	**plant like**

I planted many trees.
There is a big plantation in our area.
The show piece is plant like.

Plaster	**plaster, plasterer**	**plastered**

The mason plastered the wall slowly.
The plaster is made of lime and cement.
How can you engrave it on the plastered wall?

Play	**play, player playfulness**	**playful**

You played well.
I am a player of tennis.
Your playful nature is not good in class.

Plead	**plea, pleading pleader**	**pleading**

She pleads her case herself.
The government pleader argued our case.
The teacher helped the pleading child.

Please	**pleasure**	**pleasing pleased pleasurable**

We cannot please everyone.
It is a pleasure working with you.
We had a pleasing company.

Plump	**plumpness**	**plump**

We plumped some fruits from the orchard.
There is plumpness in his body.
He is a plump boy.

Point	**point, pointer**	**pointed**

Can you point out my mistake?
What is the point of view?
The pointed article belongs to me.

Poison	**poison**	**poisonous**

The criminal poisoned his accomplice.
There was no effect of poison on Mira.
It is a poisonous gas, stay away from it.

Polish	**polish**	**polished**

I polish my shoes daily.
There is polish in his language.
Everyone likes a polished manner.

Pollute	**pollution** **polluter**	**polluter** **pollutant**

Do not pollute the water.
What are the causes of pollution?
The pollutant agent has to be removed from the process.

Popularize	**popularization** **popularity**	**popular**

The first film popularized him.
What is the reason of his popularity?
The popular leader was given a stage to speak.

Position	**position**	**positional**

I have positioned myself well in business.
What is the position of the planets?
It was a positional move for the tycoon.

Possess	**possession** **possessor**	**possessive**

What property do you possess?
There are many flats in his possession.
My possessive nature is not good.

Post	**post**	**posted, postal**

Will you post this letter for me?
The post will arrive late today.
What is your postal address?

Powder	**powder**	**powdered** **powdery**

The grinder powdered the grains.
In summer always apply powder to the children.
The powdered material will be applied on the wall for treatment.

Practise	**practice** **practitioner**	**practised**

We must practise everyday at morning.
Practice makes a man perfect.
Practised skill can easily be noticed.

Precede	**precedence**	**precedent**

Who preceded you as the CEO?
What is the precedence is such type of projects?
Is there a precedent to welcome the interns in the company?

Precipitate	**precipitation**	**precipitate**
		precipitous

Do not precipitate the project work.

They fell in precipitation.

It is a precipitous curve.

Predict	**prediction**	**predictable**
	predictor	

I predicted this incident long back.

All your predictions about him are true.

Is it a predictable event?

Predominate	**predominance**	**predominant**

Anger should not predominate your nature.

Because of the predominance of the Mughals, other kingdoms could not progress.

Is he a predominant person in this company?

Preface	**preface**	**prefatory**

The announcer prefaced before the chief guest's speech.

Who will write the preface for my book?

What did he say in his prefatory speech?

Prefer	**preference**	**preferable**
		preferential

Do you prefer tea to coffee?

My preference is to live in a good city.

The preferential treatment should be avoided.

Prejudge	**prejudice**	**prejudice** **prejudicial**

Do not prejudge anyone?
There is no reason for prejudice here.
Your decision is prejudicial.

Prepare	**preparation** **preparedness**	**preparatory**

I will prepare them for the exam.
The preparation of the test is good.
We go to the preparatory class.

Prescribe	**prescription**	**prescriptive**

What medicine did he prescribe?
Doctor's prescription should be followed.
The prescriptive drug was effective.

Present	**presentation** **presence** **presenter**	**presentable**

He presented a miming.
When is the final presentation in the college?
Come in presentable attire for the interview.

Preserve	**preservation**	**preservative**

We must preserve our heritage.
The preservation of the building is required.
Please add some preservative in the food.

Prevent	**prevention**	**preventive** **preventable**

Will you prevent the enemy from attacking the fort?
Prevention is better than cure.
The manager took some preventive steps in the new plant.

Prickle	**prickliness**	**prickly**

The material of the new shirt prickles.
Chemical treatment will remove the prickliness from the cloth.
The prickly cloth cannot be used to make garments.

Probe	**probation** **probe**	**probationary**

The officer is probing the murder mystery.
Who is conducting the probe in this case?
The probationary officers are undergoing training.

Proceed	**procedure** **proceeding**	**procedural**

Please proceed in this work.
What is the procedure for admission in engineering?
The procedural document will be passed in the board.

Process	**process** **processor**	**processed**

I have processed the tender.
Each computer has a processor.
Do you use processed ghee?

Produce	**production**	**producible**
	producer	**productive**
	productivity	

Our company produces chemicals.
What is the production cost of this table?
We need to have some productive training.

Profess		**professed**

I profess in the art of painting.
The professed crime will be tried in front of the judge.

Programme	**programme**	**programmable**
	programmer	**programmatic**

He programmed the software very well.
What is there in the programme tomorrow?
Is it a programmable logic?

Progress	**progress**	**progressive**
	progression	

The civilization progresses on the bank of river or seashore.
There is marked progress in India.
Your progressive report is good, keep it up.

Prohibit	**prohibition**	**prohibitive**
	prohibitionist	

They will prohibit us from here.
There is prohibition on alcoholic drinks in Gujarat.
Government will take prohibitive steps against the disease.

Prolong	**prolongation**	**prolonged**

Let us prolong our stay at this hill station.

The prolongation of the departure is because of a technical fault.

This is a prolonged project that will run into loss.

Promise	**promise**	**promising**

Please promise me that you will come tomorrow.

One must keep the promise.

Your son has a promising career.

Promote	**promotion** **promoter**	**promotional**

Will you promote Ram this year?

I got a promotion in my company.

We have organized a promotional event of our new product.

Pronounce	**pronunciation** **pronouncement**	**pronounceable** **pronounced**

The judged pronounced the punishment.

What is the pronunciation of this word?

It is a pronounceable word.

Prosper	**prosperity**	**prosperous**

The city prospered owing to the visionary Mayor.

What is the reason for the prosperity of this nation?

He is son of a prosperous father.

Protect	**protection** **protector**	**protective**

Soldiers will protect the country from all kinds of invasion.
The kids are under the protection of the police.
The father has a protective attitude for children.

Protest	**protest** **protestation**	**protester**

The public will protest against the fuel price hike.
There was wide protest against the use of foreign goods.
Many protesters were arrested during the Quit India Movement.

Prove	**proof**	**provable**

Have you proved the point?
What is the proof that they will not do it again?
The provable point was cross-examined by the judge.

Provoke	**provocation**	**provocative**

Why did you provoke the public with such a remark?
The provocation of the people can lead to revolution.
Remove provocative sentences from the speech.

Pulp	**pulp, pulpiness**	**pulpy**

She will pulp the fruit to make juice.
The fruit lacks in pulpiness.
The pulpy mango was tasty.

Pulsate	**pulsation**	**pulsatory**

The heart pulsates continuously.

Look at the pulsation of the heart.

We need to check the pulsatory movement of the balloon in the machine.

Punish	**punishment**	**punishable** **punishing**

Why did you punish them?

The court gave severe punishment to the criminals.

Is it not a punishable Act?

Purge	**purgatory**	**purgatorial**

By crying he purged off his grief.

There is concept of purgatory in religion.

It was a purgatorial act.

Push	**push**	**pushing** **pushy**

Do not push me.

The push of the elephant was so strong that the whole tree fell down.

The marketing manager has a pushy manner of working.

❑

Q

VERB	NOUN	ADJECTIVE
Qualify	**qualification** **qualifier**	**qualified**

Do you qualify for the post?
What is your qualification?
The qualified candidates were called for the interview.

Quarrel	**quarrel**	**quarrelsome**

He will quarrel with neighbours for petty matters.
There was a quarrel among kids for playing.
Avoid quarrelsome persons.

Quicken	**quick**	**quickly**

Can you quicken your pace of walking?
The quick will win the race.
Come quickly, want to show you something.

Quieten	**quietness**	**quiet**

The teacher quietened the children.
The quietness of the place attracts many people.
The quiet boy was asked to speak this time.

Quote **quotation** **quotable**

I will quote Gandhiji.
There are several quotations from the *Gita*.
It is quotable line.

❑

R

VERB	NOUN	ADJECTIVE
Rain	**rain**	**rainy**

It rains heavily in Assam.
Do you like to bath in rain?
We like to move about on a rainy day.

VERB	NOUN	ADJECTIVE
Ramble	**ramble** **rambler**	**rambling**

I ramble in the hills during holidays.
My brother is a great rambler.
It is a rambling tribe.

VERB	NOUN	ADJECTIVE
Rampage	**rampage** **rampancy**	**rampant**

The mad mob rampaged the shopping centre.
There is wide rampage in the city after the kidnapping incident.
The monkeys are rampant in the village.

Reach	**reach**	**reachable**

When did you reach the office?
The goal is not out of reach.
We should first select a reachable target.

React	**reaction** **reactor**	**reactive** **reactionary**

Why did you react at his view?
There is reaction going on in the boiler.
The reactive material will be discarded.

Read	**reading** **readability**	**readable**

Let us read today's newspaper.
Reading is good for the mind.
Write in readable handwriting.

Reason	**reason**	**reasoned** **reasonable**

He reasoned out with me to join the course.
What is the reason for his failure?
Your demand is not reasonable.

Reassure	**reassurance**	**reassuring**

Please reassure them of help.
What is the reassurance from the government?
Your reassuring gesture was enough.

Rebel	**rebel, rebellion**	**rebellious**

The Indian soldiers rebelled against the British in 1857.
There was a great rebellion in French against the king.
The rebellious attitude is inborn.

Receive	**receipt, receiver**	**receivable**

You will receive a parcel soon.
Please sign the receipt.
What is the receivable in this project?

Reclaim	**reclamation**	**reclaimable**

The king reclaimed his lost territory.
The reclamation of property from bank is not easy.
Is it a reclaimable amount?

Recognize	**recognition**	**recognizable**

He recognized me.
The old man was given an award in recognition to his long service.
It is a recognizable offence.

Rectify	**rectification** **rectifier**	**rectifiable**

How will you rectify your mistake?
He took this step in rectification of the technical error.
It is not a rectifiable mistake done by the machine.

Recur	**recurrence**	**recurrent** **recurring**

Fever recurs every month.
As there was recurrence of fever, he consulted a senior doctor.
The recurrent fever has to be cured anyhow.

Redden	**redness**	**red, reddish**

His face reddened because of anger.
There is redness in the sky during dusk.
Do you like that red dress?

Redeem	**redeem** **redemption**	**redeemable**

I want to redeem my shares.
The redemption of mankind is in the hands of God.
These debenture are redeemable after one year.

Reduce	**reduction**	**reducible** **reductive**

You need to reduce your weight.
There is reduction in the price of onions.
The government took reductive measure for the price.

Refer	**reference**	**referable** **referential**

I have referred to Shakespeare in my speech.
This is in reference to your talk with my partner.
We are looking for referential membership in the club.

Refine	**refinement** **refiner**	**refined**

The plant refines oil.
There is refinement in his manners.
Use only refined oil in eating.

Reflect	**reflection** **reflector**	**reflective**

You should reflect on your actions.
There is reflection of dog on the water.
I think a lot when in reflective mood.

Reform	**reformation** **reformer**	**reformative** **reformatory**

The father reformed all the sons well.
Our Government must take some steps for reformation.
What reformative steps shall we take?

Refract	**refraction** **refractor**	**refractive**

The light refracted due to the mirror.
This happens due to refraction.
What is the refractive index of light?

Refresh	**refreshment** **refresher**	**refreshing**

They will refresh the students in break.
Will you attend the refresher course?
The cold water was refreshing.
He sang refreshingly for the audience.

Refrigerate	**refrigeration** **refrigerator**	**refrigerant**

You should refrigerate the vegetables to avoid decay.
Refrigeration keeps eatables cool and fresh.
It is a refrigerant gas.

Refund	**refund**	**refundable**

Will you refund our fees?
What is the amount of refund?
The refundable sum was paid in his account.

Regard	**regard**	**regardless** **regardful**

I regard him a good man.
The students have high regards for the professor.
He will come regardless of the weather.

Regret	**regret**	**regretful**

Do not regret on spilt milk.
He asked for forgiveness out of regret.
The regretful man began to weep.

Regulate	**regulation** **regulator**	**regulatory**

The government has regulated the price of salt.
What is the regulation about taking leaves?
We need some regulatory measures to curb delays in work.

Relate	**relation** **relative**	**related**

Please relate the incident to us.
What is your relation with me?
The related documents have to be submitted in the office.

Relax	**relaxation**	**relaxed**

I will relax on Sunday.
The Yoga teacher explained the techniques of relaxation.
The manager's relaxed attitude perplexed us.

Rely	**reliance** **reliability**	**reliable**

Whom do you rely on for this work?
Let us test the reliability of this machine.
The reliable employee is in demand in all teams.

Remark	**remark**	**remarkable**

What did the principal remark on your presentation?
I like your remark on the budget.
Sardar Patel was a remarkable man.

Remove	**removal**	**removable**

Please remove this item from the list.
The removal of waste cannot be in this area.
Is it a removable part of the machine?

Renew	**renewal**	**renewable**

I renewed my membership in the club.
What is the renewal charge?
Today we are after renewable energy.

Repair	**repair, repairer**	**repairable**

He has repaired his scooter.
The repair was not so good so again it is not working.
It is not a repairable loss.

Repeat	**repeater** **repetition**	**repeatable** **repetitious** **repetitive**

Do not repeat such silly mistake.
There is lot of repetition of the same idea in the essay.
Remove the repetitive words.

Repose	**repose**	**reposeful**
	reposition	

The traveller reposed at an inn.
A good repose will refresh you for onward journey.
The reposeful time gave me a lot of energy.

Represent	**representation**	**representative**

Whom do you represent in the meeting?
There was a representation from the students' federation.
He is a representative of our government.

Repress	**repression**	**repressed**

Do not repress your feelings for her.
Army was called for repression of the riots.
The repressed thought all of a sudden found a voice.

Reproach	**reproach**	**reproachful**

The father will reproach you if you do it.
There is no effect on him of the reproach.
Father's reproachful nature is not good for the development of children.

Repudiate	**repudiation**	**repulsive**

On what base did you repudiate their claim?
There is no concrete reason behind the repudiation of the plan.
He has a repulsive nature.

Require	**requirement**	**requisite**

What do you require to complete this project in time?
We must understand their requirements first.
Please fill up the requisite form for the admission.

Resent	**resentment**	**resentful**

Do not resent the child.
He blasted on him out of resentment.
He has some resentful colleagues.

Reserve	**reservation**	**reserved**

Will you reserve seats for us?
There is a form to be filled for reservation.
How many tables are reserved?

Reside	**residence, resident**	**residential**

Where do your reside?
He is a residence of New Delhi.
What is your residential address?

Resign	**resignation**	**resigned**

When did he resign?
Your resignation is not accepted by the management.
The resigned employees were called by the manager.

Resist	**resistance** **resistor**	**resistant**

The mob resisted the *lathi charge* of the police.
There is no resistance from the public for price hike.
We need a resistant spirit to fight evil.

Resolve	**resolution**	**resolute** **resolved**

I have resolved to complete the mission.
What is your New Year resolution?
Gandhi was a resolute man.

Respect	**respect**	**respectable**
	respecter	**respectful**
	respectability	

Whom do you respect the most at home?

To get respect you must give respect.

Any respectable citizen will not do such a work.

Respire	**respiration**	**respiratory**
	respirator	

Plants respire more in daylight.

We get oxygen from plants because of their respiration.

What are the respiratory organs?

Respond	**response**	**respondent**

Did he respond to your letter?

What is the response of the management in terms of the production problems?

The respondent has filed an answer.

Restore	**restoration**	**restorative**
	restorer	

We should restore the glory of India.

The restoration of the fort was done by archaeological department.

This is a regular restorative work.

Restrict	**restriction**	**restrictive**

Why do you restrict the children in doing so?

Is there any restriction on visiting the fort?

Government can take restrictive steps against monopoly.

Result	**result**	**resultant**

His laziness resulted into failure in exam.
What is the result of the match between India and England?
We predicted the resultant action from the management.

Resume	**resumption**	**resumptive**

He resumed office from today after taking a vacation.
What is the resumption process in government offices?
It is a resumptive function for me.

Retaliate	**retaliation**	**retaliatory**

Do not retaliate blindly.
The army fired several rounds at the terrorists in retaliation.
The retaliatory action was not appreciated by the minister.

Retard	**retardation**	**retarded** **retardant**

The recession retarded growth of many companies.
The retardation damaged the life of the boy.
The retarded children are under treatment.

Retire	**retirement**	**retired**

Everyone retires from service at sixty.
What is your plan for retirement?
The retired officers were invited as consultants and teachers.

Retrieve	**retrieval**	**retrievable**

We could not retrieve some money from the debtor.
What is the retrieval procedure in the bank?
The retrievable amount will be deposited in your account.

Reveal	**revelation**	**revealing**

What does nature reveal to us?
The revelation of the truth surprised all.
Do not put on a revealing dress.

Revenge	**revenge**	**revengeful**

Rana Pratap revenged the Mughals by attacking their forts.
What will you get from this revenge?
Do not be revengeful.

Reverberate	**reverberation**	**reverberant**

The crowd reverberated the slogan of the leader.
The valley made noise in reverberation.
The reverberant point is visited by all tourists.

Reverse	**reversion**	**reversible**

How will you reverse this process?
He collided with a tree in reversion.
It is not a reversible process.

Revert	**reversion**	**revertible**

When will you revert to me with an answer?
There has been reversion of the development of this company.
Your step is revertible.

Revoke	**revocation**	**revocable**

The Parliament revoked the bill.
The government took this step in revocation.
Is it a revocable procedure?

Reward **reward** **rewarding**

We rewarded him for his work.
What did you get as reward?
Meeting the great man was a rewarding experience for me.

Riot **riot, rioter** **riotous**

The people of this area riot every now and then.
What was the cause of the communal riot?
The riotous action was soon curbed by the police force.

Ripen **ripeness** **ripe**

When will the mangoes ripen?
There was ripeness in his behaviour.
We want only ripe mangoes.

Risk **risk, riskiness** **risky**

He risked his asset in the share market.
Why do you want to take such a risk?
The risky plan was put aside.

Roast **roaster** **roasted**

We will roast some peanuts for breakfast.
Put the food on the roaster.
Give me some roasted bread.

Root **root** **rootless, rooted**

Several tribes rooted in this region.
How long are the roots of the Banyan tree!
Is it a rootless plant?

Rotate **rotation** **rotable, rotatory rotational**

Do not rotate the wheels like this.
How many rotations are there of this fan?
The machine is making sound owing to the rotational movement of the belt.

Rough **roughness** **rough roughish**

He was roughed up by the police.
There is roughness on the table.
The rough surface must be polished again.

Ruin **ruin, ruination** **ruinous**

Drinking ruined him and his family.
What did you see in the ruins of the fort?
Tobacco is a ruinous habit.

Rumble **rumble** **rumbustious**

The car rumbled through the area.
The rumble of the vehicle was heard till far owing to silence.
The new machine is rumbustious.

Ruminate **rumination** **ruminative**

Do not ruminate much about that problem.
He was lost in rumination of the matter.
His ruminative habit is good till a certain extent.

❑

S

VERB	NOUN	ADJECTIVE
Salvage	**salvage**	**salvageable**

The saint salvaged them from making sins.
It took time in salvage of the destitute.
Is it a salvageable place?

Satiate	**satiation**	**satiable**

You can satiate your hunger with this food.
A glass of cool water gave me satiation.
Lord Ganesh did not have a satiable hunger once.

Satire	**satirist, satire**	**satirical**

The poet satirized his rivals in the new poem.
Pope was a great satirist.
He wrote many satirical verses.

Satisfy	**satisfaction**	**satisfactory**

Did the new salary structure satisfy your wants?
We should try for satisfaction in life.
It was a satisfactory experience.

Save	**saving, saver**	**saveable**

We must save the environment.
Always have the habit of saving money.
It is not a saveable product.

Scar	**scar**	**scarred**

The fall scarred his leg.
What is the scar on his right hand?
His image is scarred in the organization after this news.

Scare	**scare**	**scarred**

Don't scare away the birds.
The children screamed in scare.
The scarred child ran to the mother and started crying.

Scatter	**scatter**	**scattered**

You can scatter the marbles here for the children to play.
There was a scatter of toys in the room.
The scattered soldiers were summoned at one place to start the march.

Scent	**scent**	**scented**

He scents his chamber everyday.
The scent of this flower is sweet.
Please give me a scented item.

Scheme	**scheme**	**scheming**

What is he scheming against the government?
The scheme of rural employment is doing well.
The scheming politician was arrested by the police.

School	**school**	**schooled**

I schooled from a small town.
Where is your school?
The schooled kids were better mannered than the others.

Scorch	**scorch**	**scorching**

The sun scorched terribly in summer.
He fell unconscious owing to the scorch of the sun.
The scorching heat does not allow people to move out of their homes.

Scrap	**scrap**	**scrappy**

He scrapped the plan because of high budget.
There is lot of scrap in the ship.
The scrappy parts were gathered on the ground.

Scratch	**scratch** **scratchiness**	**scratchy**

He scratched the card to get the pin number.
There is a scratch on the door.
It is a scratchy surface.

Scrawl	**scrawl**	**scrawly**

The officer scrawled a few lines for documentation.
I have noted some points in my scrawl.
Your handwriting looks scrawly.

Search	**search** **searcher**	**searching**

I am searching for my lost pen.
When shall we begin the search for a new CEO?
The searching committee will be formed soon.

Season	**seasoning**	**seasoned**

He has seasoned himself as a businessman.
The seasoning of the cricket bat calls for a particular process.
Take when you deal with a seasoned person.

Secrete	**secretion**	**secretory**

It secretes sugar in the body.
Secretion of fat will not take place with this medicine.
Which are the secretory organs in the body?

Secure	**security**	**secured**

Did you secure the first position?
The security office is at the gate.
We do not have to worry for the secured person.

See	**sight**	**sighted** **sightless**

What do you see from here?
It was a dreadful sight.
He reads books at evening for the sightless.

Seed	**seed**	**seedless**

The non-violent freedom movement of India seeded in the mind of Mahatma Gandhi.
A tree will come out of the seed.
How did you grow a seedless fruit?

Select	**selection** **selector**	**selective**

Why did you select this course?
What is the selection procedure of raw material?
He is very selective about food.

Sense	**sense, sensibility**	**sensible**

He sensed a danger in the jungle.
He is a person of fine sensibility.
What a sensible man!

Separate	**separation**	**separated**
	separateness	

Will you separate the two materials?
There was separation of the couple.
The separated couple is fighting for the right of the son.

Shade	**shade, shadiness**	**shady**
Shadow	**shadow**	**shadowy**

The tree shadowed in the compound.
Look at the fearsome shadow of a tree.
It is a shadowy area.

Shame	**shame**	**shameful**
	shamefulness	**shameless**

Your behaviour shamed us all.
It was a shame on the entire family.
The shameless boy was punished by the father.

Shape	**shape**	**shapeless**
	shapelessness	**shapely**
	shapeliness	

Are you shaping your future well?
What is the shape of this article?
He has developed a shapely figure.

Sharpen **sharpness, sharpener** **sharp**

Teach the children to sharpen their skills.
The sharpness of the knife is dangerous.
There was a sharp pain on his hand.

Shave **shave, shaver** **shaven**

I shave at morning.
The barber good a good return for shave from the king.
He looks good with a shaven beard.

Shell **shell** **shell-like**

The fighter planes shelled the border area of enemy country.
What do you get from a shell?
It is a shell-like boat.

Shock **shock** **shocking**

He was shocked on seeing blood.
The shock of earthquake was terrible on the people.
What shocking news!

Shower **shower** **showery**

The king showered gifts on the clever man.
We took a shower in the morning.
It was a showery evening of monsoon.

Shrink **shrinkage** **shrunken**

His health will still shrink if there is no proper medication.
The shrinkage of the cloth is its typical characteristic.
Remove the shrunken material from the barrel.

Shy **shyness** **shy**

He will shy in talking in front of many people.
Shyness is not good quality in a professional.
The shy boy was encouraged by the teacher to speak.

Sicken **sickening** **sickeningly**

The heat sickens us.
It was a sickening experience in the sea.
He went into the hospital sickeningly.

Side **side** **side**

I will side him the competition.
Whose side are you taking?
The side window is open.

Signify **significance** **significant**
signification

What does this colour signify?
What is the significance of this instrument?
It was a significant event in the history of India.

Sin **sin, sinner** **sinful**

Do not sin.
The sinner will be punished today or tomorrow.
Killing him with treachery was sinful.

Sit **seat, sitter** **sitting**

Do not sit here.
What is the seat number?
The sitting MP was invited as the chief guest.

Sizzle	**sizzle**	**sizzling**

The rain sizzled against the glass.
Do not be afraid. It is the noise of the sizzle owing to wind.
What sizzling heat is it!

Sketch	**sketch**	**sketchy**

Can you sketch with pencil?
What a beautiful sketch of the queen!
I have a sketchy memory of that person.

Skin	**skin**	**skinless**

The cook skinned the vegetables to cook.
What is the colour of his skin?
The fruits are skinless.

Slacken	**slackness**	**slack**

The business slackened owing to economic recession.
There is slackness in his gait.
The slack company was shut down by the management.

Sleep	**sleep, sleeper sleepiness**	**sleepy**

How long will you sleep?
I had a good sleep yesterday.
The sleepy dog found a place to sleep under a tree.

Sleet	**sleet**	**sleety**

It is sleeting outside.

The vehicles could not travel in the region because of the sleet.

It was a sleety night yesterday.

Slight	**slightness**	**slight**

Do not slight anyone, it is not good.
Slightness of change will not be helpful here.
There was a slight movement there.

Slim	**slimming, slimmer**	**slim**

He is slimming because of exercise.
The slimming of the body calls for diet control and exercise.
Look at that slim man.

Slip	**slip**	**slip, slippery**

The walled slipped from my hand.
He was injured because of the slip of bike.
Take care of the slippery floor.

Slope	**slope** **sloppiness**	**sloppy**

The building slopes towards the East.
Do not drive fast on the slope.
You must take care on the sloppy road.

Slow	**slowness**	**slow**

Please slow down the car.
Slowness in walking will not give you exercise.
We cannot take into the team any slow player.

Smoke	**smoke, smokiness**	**smoky**

Do you smoke?
The smoke was seen from far.
There was a smoky atmosphere on the hills.

Smooth **smoothness** **smooth**

The carpenters are smoothing the table.
The table has a wonderful smoothness.
Do not run on the smooth floor.

Sneer **sneer** **sneering**

I sneered at him in irritation.
The king's sneer is very dangerous.
The sneering dog was stoned by the people.

Snoop **snooper** **snoopy**

Do not snoop in this matter.
He was a snooper of the college.
Your snoopy nature is disliked by all.

Solve **solution** **solvable**

Will you solve this
What is the solution of this technical problem?
Is it a solvable mathematical sum?

Sorrow **sorrow** **sorrowful**

Do not sorrow for him.
I understand your sorrow.
He looked at us with a sorrowful eye.

Sound **sound** **soundless**

You can sound the alarm if the ship tosses on the waves.
What is that sound?
It was a dark and soundless night.

Sour	**sourness**	**sour**

The cook soured the dish for experiment.
There is more sourness in this food.
The grapes are sour.

Spare	**sparseness**	**spare**

Why did you spare the culprit?
Sparseness is not good for crime.
This is a spare part of the car.

Spark	**spark**	**sparkling**

The wood sparked at night.
The fire happened because of the spark.
It was a sparkling diamond.

Spike	**spike, spikiness**	**spiky**

Thorns spiked out near the lawn.
We need shoes with spikes.
It was a spiky surface.

Spot	**spot, spottiness**	**spotless**
	spotter	**spotty**

Can you spot any difference?
At what spot are they meeting?
I want to develop a spotless character.

Star	**star, stardom**	**starry**

Who stars in your next film?
After achieving stardom, he became proud.
It was a starry diamond shop.

Stick	**sticker, stickiness**	**sticky**

How will you stick the posters?
The sticker is there behind the seat.
My hands are sticky, I need to wash them.

Stimulate	**stimulation** **stimulator**	**stimulant** **stimulator**

Why did you stimulate his temper?
He did the deed in stimulation.
This medicine works as stimulant.

String	**string**	**stringed**

The serial strings into many episodes.
Tie the bundle with a strong string.
The stringed bird could not fly.

Study	**study**	**studied**

Do not study in heat.
We have a room in the house for study.
There was a studied expression on his face.

Submit	**submission**	**submissive**

Who will you submit the file?
We have submission of the project work in college tomorrow.
He wife has a submissive nature.

Succeed	**success**	**successful**

How did you succeed in the final?
We should work very hard for success in our field.
I know a successful person who can guide us.

Suggest	**suggestion**	**suggestible** **suggestive**

What do you suggest about the picnic?

I liked your suggestion.

The manager's suggestive remark was understood by the guard.

Suit	**suitability**	**suitable**

Will it suit your requirement?

There is no suitability in this pair.

Is it not a suitable cloth?

Supervise	**supervision** **supervisor**	**supervisory**

Let us not supervise them, they are experienced.

There is not supervisory control in this factory.

Supply	**supply** **supplement** **supplier**	**supplementary**

Did he supply the goods in time?

Who is your supplier of raw materials?

The university has arranged a supplementary exam.

Support	**support, supporter** **supportiveness**	**supportive**

Why didn't you support me?

We have some good supporters during this election.

I appreciate your supportive nature.

Suppress	**suppression** **suppressor**	**suppressible**

Do not suppress your feelings for her, go and tell her.
Suppression of the naxalite activities is necessary.
It is not a suppressible feeling.

Surprise	**surprise**	**surprising**

He surprised me by coming early.
What a pleasant surprise!
We had a surprising evening with old friends.

Suspend	**suspension**	**suspended**

The management will suspend the peon for his negligence.
Did you get the suspension orders?
The suspended police officer was called back to duty owing to unrest in the city.

Sustain	**sustenance**	**sustainable**

How will you sustain the business with so low capital?
The sustenance of business calls for good management.
We are looking forward for a sustainable growth.

Swank	**swank**	**swanky**

The boys swank their mobiles and bikes.
He spent a lot of his father's money for swank.
Wow! What a swanky car!

Swell	**swelling**	**swollen**

The profit of the money lender swelled in the village.
There is a swelling on the hand.
You must treat you swollen ear quickly.

❑

T

VERB	NOUN	ADJECTIVE
Talk	**talk, talker**	**talkative**

I will talk to them for this matter.
We had a talk on the project.
He is very talkative.

VERB	NOUN	ADJECTIVE
Tangle	**tangle**	**tangled**

The puzzle tangled the kids.
The rope is in a tangle, cannot be untied.
The tangled rope had to be cut.

VERB	NOUN	ADJECTIVE
Taste	**taste, taster tastiness tastelessness**	**tasteful tasteless, tasty**

What did you taste in the restaurant?
How is the taste of the cake?
The drink is tasteless.

VERB	NOUN	ADJECTIVE
Tax	**tax, taxation**	**taxable**

The government is taxing the new factories.
What is the slab of taxation for senior citizens?
Is it a taxable income?

Teach	**teacher, teaching**	**teachable**

Do not teach me mathematics.
He is an English teacher.
It is not a teachable matter.

Telephone	**telephone**	**telephonic**

We telephoned the office to inquire.
Where is the telephone wire in the room?
As per our telephonic conversation we will meet at evening.

Test	**test**	**testable**

I am testing his skills of driving.
We have a test of English Grammar today.
The chemical is testable in laboratory.

Thank	**thank**	**thankful** **thankless**

Do not thank me for this.
No gift, just thanks is enough.
He is a thankless person, don't help him.

Think	**thought, thinker** **thoughtfulless**	**thoughtful** **thoughtless**

What do you think about the programme?
Please share your thought about the HR budget.
His thoughtless action ruined him.

Thunder	**thunder**	**thundery** **thunderous**

The big man thundered in the room with a shout.
The thunder was frightening the children.
It was a thunderous evening of August.

Tickle **tickle** — **tickly, ticklish**

The grass tickled our feet as we walked.
He put a bandage where the cloth tickled.
The ticklish sensation is due to the cream.

Time **time, timeliness** **timely**

The batsman timed the short very well.
What time is it now?
The timely delivery of the raw material saved a lot of hassles.

Tire **tiredness** **tired**

The long journey tired them.
He slept early owing to tiredness.
My tired body was asking for water and food.

Torture **torture, torturer** **torturous**

Why do you torture your wife like this?
He could not bear the torture and committed suicide.
It was a torturous treatment for the prisoners.

Trace **trace** **traceable**

The guards traced the tiger in the forest.
There is no trace of the missing necklace.
These marks on the mud are traceable.

Transfer **transfer, transference** **transferable**

The bank transferred me to a bigger branch with promotion.
Why did the transfer of money take so long?
Is your job transferable?

Transmit	**transmission** **transmitter**	**transmissible** **transmittable**

Let us transmit the message through wireless.
There is a transmission tower near our house.
These sound waves are not transmissible.

Travel	**travelling, traveller**	**travelled**

How did you travel here?
He is tireless traveller of desert.
I opted for less travelled path.

Treat	**treatment**	**treatable**

Please treat the guests well.
What treatment has the doctor recommended?
Cancer is not a treatable disease.

Trick	**trick, trickery** **trickster** **trickiness**	**tricky**

He tricked us for doing this.
Do not play trick on us.
We must come out of this tricky situation.

Triumph	**triumph**	**triumphal** **triumphant**

The team triumphed easily.
We celebrated the triumph with all.
The triumphant team was felicitated by the government.

Trouble	**trouble**	**troublesome**

Why do you trouble him every now and then?
We must help him to come out of trouble.
He has a troublesome attitude.

Trust	**trust**	**trusting**
	trustworthiness	**trustworthy**

Do you trust me?
We appreciate his trustworthiness.
All of us need a trustworthy friend.

Twang	**twang**	**twangy**

The chimes twanged in the breeze.
The rod fell with a loud twang.
The constant twangy noise is disturbing.

Twinkle	**twinkle**	**twinkly**

Stars twinkled in the sky at night.
Can you see twinkle in the sky?
It is a twinkly diamond.

Twitter	**twitter**	**twittery**

The little bird twitters at morning.
I like to listen to the twitter of birds in the morning.
The door bell has a twittery sound.

Tyrannize	**tyranny, tyrant**	**tyrannous**

The dictator tyrannizes the people in his country.
Hitler was a tyrant.
People fled the country because of the dictator's tyrannous behaviour.

❑

U

VERB	NOUN	ADJECTIVE
Understand	**understanding**	**understandable** **understanding**

Do you understand the value of time?
All depends on your understanding.
The problem is understandable.

Undo	**undoing**	**undone**

I will undo this work.
The scratch is because of the undoing of the work.
The undone work need not be remembered.

Undress	**undress**	**undressed**

I undressed to plunge into the swimming pool.
This undress is not descent.
The boys jumped into the pool undressed.

Unify	**unification**	**unified**

I cannot unify the two rival companies.
The unification of Germany was a historical event.
The unified people fought the evil government.

Uplift	**uplift**	**uplifting**

Let us uplift the poor of the area with education.
The uplift of the poor is the prime focus of the government.
The uplifting people were educated first.

Upset	**upset**	**upset**

Do not upset me with your nonsense.
The upset in the tournament was shocking for the public.
The upset mind cannot think much.

Use	**use, usefulness** **uselessness**	**useful** **useless**

What will you use to prepare this material?
Each item has its usefulness.
The useless material was discarded.

❑

V

VERB	NOUN	ADJECTIVE
Vacate	**vacancy**	**vacant**

They will vacate our house next month.
Is there a vacancy of marketing executive in your company?
The vacant posts were advertised in the newspaper.

Value	**value, valuer** **valuation**	**valuable** **valueless**

Does he value time?
What is the value of this obligation?
The valuable stone was kept in the locker of the bank.

Vary	**variation** **variability**	**variable** **variant**

How did this sample vary?
There is slight variation between the products.
The variable figure looks big.

Veil	**veil**	**veiled**

The queen veiled her face as soon as she entered the court.
We require big veil to be put here.
The veiled queen sat beside the king.

Venerate	**veneration** **venerator**	**venerable**

Do you venerate your parents?
We stood up in veneration of the Chief Justice.
The venerable man was welcomed everywhere.

Venture	**venture**	**venturesome**

He ventures into many businesses.
We want to support her venture.
A venturesome entrepreneur can win success.

Verify	**verification**	**verifiable**

Please verify the details.
There is a process of verification that has to be carried out.
We did not find any verifiable item.

Vex	**vexation**	**vexatious, vexed**

He vexes his sister at home.
The audience moved out in vexation.
The vexed man started shouting at the officer in bank.

Vibrate	**vibration, vibrator** **vibrancy**	**vibrant** **vibratory**

The phone vibrates on the table.
The vibration was very powerful.
Who does not like a vibrant manager?

Vindicate	**vindication** **vindicator**	**vindictive** **vindicatory**

He tried to vindicate himself before the judge.
The vindicator suffered a lot.
It was a vindictive step.

Violate **violation, violator** **violable**

Did you violate some norms?

Violation of the rules of the institute is not good.

Such rules are violable and therefore we have to take care of it.

Visualize **visualization, vision** **visual**

I could visualize the disaster.

Psychiatrist has prescribed exercises of visualization.

Do you use visual aids in the presentation?

❑

W

VERB	NOUN	ADJECTIVE
Wake	**wakefulness**	**wakeful**

Did the noise wake you up?
The guard did not miss any sight in wakefulness.
The wakeful sentry caught hold of the thief.

Walk	**walk, walker**	**walkable**

Let us walk in the garden.
Shall we go for a walk in the garden?
My house is at a walkable distance.

Wall	**wall**	**walled**

The king walled the entire area to protect against invasion.
The wall of the fort is high and strong.
We live in walled city.

Want	**want**	**wanted, wanting**

Do you want water?
We should work for our wants.
The wanted criminal was nabbed from the village.

Warm	**warmth**	**warm**

I will warm the water for your bath.
There was warmth in friend's words.
We got a warm welcome at their place.

Wash	**wash, washer** **washing**	**washable**

Will you wash your hands before lunch?
I will go for a wash in the morning.
Is it a washable material?

Waste	**wastage, waste**	**wasteful**

Do not waste water.
There is lot of wastage of water in our area.
What a wasteful boy!

Watch	**watch, watcher** **watchfulness**	**watchable** **watchful**

We would like to watch the movements of the animals in the forest.
To be a good manager, you need watchfulness.
It is not a watchable film.

Wax	**wax**	**wax**

Please wax my shoes properly.
Candles are made of wax.
How many wax statues are there in the museum?

Weaken	**weakness** **weakling**	**weak**

Illness has weakened him much.
He had to take rest owing to weakness.
We should help the weak.

Weary	**weariness**	**weary** **wearisome**

The long walk wearied us.
He sat down on the bench out of weariness.
The weary man was looking for water to drink.

Wed	**wedding**	**wedded**

Whom did she wed?
We will attend their wedding.
The wedded couple was blessed by the elders.

Weed	**weed**	**weedy**

The farmers will weed out the thorns.
The weed will harm the crop.
It was a weedy farm.

Weigh	**weight** **weightiness**	**weighty** **weightiness**

How much does he weigh?
My weight is 65 kgs.
The child has become weighty.

Wheeze	**wheeziness**	**wheezy**

The athlete wheezed after practice.
His wheeziness needs treatment.
The wheezy boy was asked to sit down for a while.

Whiten	**whiteness**	**white**
	whitener	**whitish**

He whitened the entire lobby of the building.
Why is there whiteness in this material?
I like white shirt.

Widen	**width**	**wide**

The municipality will widen the roads.
What is the width of this table?
This angle is wide.

Wiggle	**wiggle**	**wiggly**

The servant wiggled the wet cloth.
The wiggle will tear the cloth.
His movement is wiggly.

Win	**winner**	**winnable**

They will win the race this time.
Who was declared the winner of the quiz?
Is it not a winnable game?

Wing	**wing**	**winged**

The hawk winged through the clouds quickly.
All birds have two wings.
Have you seen a winged animal?

Wish	**wish**	**wishful**

What do you wish to do after school?
Your wish is my command.
It is not a wishful thinking but a reality.

Withdraw	**withdrawal**	**withdrawn**

I want to withdraw some money from the bank.
The withdrawal of support by the allies was at a wrong time.
What will you do with the withdrawn money?

Wonder	**wonderment** **wonder**	**wonderful**

I wondered at the great monument.
The child gazed at the sky in wonderment.
What a wonderful human being!

Work	**work, workability** **worker**	**workable** **working**

Will you work till late?
We must complete the work in time.
It is a workable budget.

Wrinkle	**wrinkle**	**wrinkly**

He wrinkled the waste paper and threw it.
There is not wrinkle on his face still.
The old lady's hand is wrinkly.

Wrong	**wrongness** **wrongdoer** **wrongdoing**	**wrong** **wrongful**

Did he wrong you again?
Your wrongdoing will be punished by God.
It was a wrong decision.

❑

Y

VERB	NOUN	ADJECTIVE
Yap	**yap**	**yappy**

The puppy yapped from behind.
The yap of the puppy was hardly heard outside.
The yappy dogs are ferocious.

VERB	NOUN	ADJECTIVE
Yellow	**yellowness**	**yellow** **yellowish** **yellowy**

Jaundice yellowed his eyes.
There is yellowness in the dress.
The yellowish chemical is costly.

VERB	NOUN	ADJECTIVE
Yield	**yield**	**yielding**

You will yield good result from this.
The yield this year is very good.
The yielding man is considered a coward.